"All right, campers." Mr. O., who had been helping some kids in the back of the room, was standing next to their lab table. "What seems to be the problem here?"

"Nothing," Maggie said, hoping Mr. O. hadn't overheard their conversation. She wanted to have her thoughts all worked out before she explained to him—tried to explain to him—why she wouldn't be doing the dissection on Friday.

"We were having a philosophical discussion," Matt said loftily.

"I touched my worm again," Maggie said, wondering if Mr. O. would give her another approving smile. He did, and Maggie once more basked in the glow of his good opinion. Then he moved on to another lab table.

It had been a momentous morning, all right.

Maggie had touched a worm.

And she had become a vegetarian.

Also by Claudia Mills

Dinah Forever

Losers, Inc.

Standing Up to Mr. O.

Claudia Mills

SCHOLASTIC INC.
New York Toronto London Auckland Sydney
Mexico City New Delhi Hong Kong

ISBN 0-439-17372-8

Text copyright © 1998 by Claudia Mills.
Cover images copyright © 2000 by Jim Carroll.
All rights reserved.
Published by Scholastic Inc., 555 Broadway, New York, NY 10012,
by arrangement with Hyperion Books for Children,
an imprint of Buena Vista Books, Inc.
SCHOLASTIC and associated logos are trademarks
and/or registered trademarks of Scholastic Inc.

12 11 10 9 8 7 6 5 4 3 2 1   0 1 2 3 4 5/0

Printed in the U.S.A.   40

First Scholastic printing, October 2000

To Elaine Chubb,
who shows (again)
that copyediting can be exquisite

Standing Up
to Mr. O.

1

Mr. O. was wearing Maggie McIntosh's favorite tie, the one that looked like an enormous, bright yellow Crayola crayon. Seated on top of his desk, he waited for the bell to finish ringing. Then he grinned down at the fourth-period, seventh-grade biology class. Maggie felt as if he were smiling especially at her.

"Okay, campers, winter break is over, the new year has begun, and I want you to tell me: How many psychiatrists does it take to change a light bulb?"

Maggie waited expectantly, not even trying to guess the answer. She wasn't good at jokes or riddles, and she didn't know anything about psychiatrists. She didn't think anyone in their class had ever been to a psychiatrist, except maybe Jake Dycus, whose black leather jacket and sullen silence made him seem like the stereotype of a "troubled" kid. But Maggie loved Mr. O.'s light bulb jokes, anyway. Even after four months, Mr. O. hadn't run out of them. It was another reason why Mr. O. was Maggie's favorite teacher, maybe even her favorite human being.

No one called out an answer. Then Mr. O. said, "One . . . but the light bulb has to really *want* to change."

He laughed, and Maggie laughed with him, even though she wasn't sure why the joke was funny. Mr. O. had such an infectious chuckle that she wanted to laugh whenever he did.

Sharing Maggie's lab table, the middle one in the front row, Matt Dixon tapped impatiently on his opened notebook with his pencil as if to say, Are we finished with joke time yet? Matt never laughed at any of Mr. O.'s jokes. Jokes were beneath him.

Mr. O. glanced at Matt. "Moving right along," he said, "today in Camp Biology we begin the study of Annelida." He jumped down lightly from his desk and wrote the word on the board in his bold, clear handwriting. "The phylum of segmented worms."

Maggie turned around to look at her best friend, Alycia Eagen, who sat with Kip Edwards at the lab table right behind hers. Maggie knew that Alycia had been dreading the worm unit as much as she had. Both girls had hated worms for as many years as they had been friends, ever since they had stood together on the playground on rainy days back in second grade, shrieking whenever they saw a worm writhing on the wet black-top. But Alycia's face managed to show only intelligent interest in whatever Mr. O. was going to say next.

"This is also the week," Mr. O. said in the matter-of-fact, business-as-usual voice that he used to drop major bombshells, such as the time he announced that half the class had failed the last exam. "This is also the week we will do our first dissection."

Kip Edwards called out, "Are we going to dissect a *worm*?"

Mr. O. paused for effect. Then he grinned. "We are."

Maggie felt a shock of dread. She had known when she signed up for biology that they were going to do dissections, but biology was a required subject, so she hadn't had any choice except to take it. And once the course began, back in September, Maggie had loved it, and Mr. O., so much that she had let herself forget the inevitable, half convincing herself that maybe Mr. O. would forget, too.

There was no way Maggie could dissect a worm. There was no way she could kill a living thing and cut it up into tiny pieces. She would have to explain it to Mr. O., and he would understand, as he did the time she'd panicked before the first biology test, when he had been so patient and encouraging. Or the time she had told him about her father.

She focused back on the present. The class was still registering its reaction to Mr. O.'s announcement. Some of the other girls looked as ill as Maggie felt, but some of the boys were cheering. Kip Edwards was pantomiming chopping up a worm with what appeared to be a machete. Jake Dycus looked even more sullen and surly than usual. Matt wore his trademark expression of superior disdain.

"They're being pretty infantile, don't you think?" Matt finally said to Maggie. Because Maggie was as good a student as Matt, occasionally he was willing to speak to her as an equal.

Maggie nodded. How could anybody cheer at the idea of *killing* something? Even though Maggie hated worms, she would never want to see one killed, destroyed, its small, insignificant existence snuffed out.

"These kids need to get a life," Matt went on. "Medical students dissect *corpses.* It's all part of science. Medical students don't cheer about it or gag about it; they just do it because it's the best way to learn about the human body."

Maggie greatly doubted that people in medical school never gagged at the sight of a corpse. Medical students probably fainted onto the floor on a regular basis. But she didn't want to be drawn into an extended conversation with Matt. She wanted it to be September again, with the prospect of dissections far in the distant future.

Mr. O. let the commotion go on for another minute. Then he blew on the whistle that he wore around his neck to show that he was the head counselor for Camp Biology.

"Listen, campers," Mr. O. said. "I know this will be a new experience for most of you, maybe for all of you." His voice had become gentle, and even though Maggie was staring down at her desk, she could tell that he was looking at her as he spoke. "Remember, we're all in Camp Biology together. If you're nervous about your first dissection, your lab partner will help you, or I'll help you. Most people are a bit scared and squeamish the first time. But we're all going to get through this. Okay? Okay."

Maggie felt a little better, because Mr. O.'s tone was so calm and reassuring, but not much better.

"We will dissect an earthworm on Friday," Mr. O. went on. "Today I want you to begin getting to know your worms."

With a flourish, he whisked the cover off the large glass terrarium that stood on a rolling table next to his desk. "Our class worm farm," he announced. The terrarium was filled almost to the top with moist dirt. Maggie thought she could see *something* tunneling through the dirt. Quickly she averted her eyes.

"Every pair of lab partners will get its very own worm," Mr. O. said. "One of these glass jars"—he pointed to a row of mayonnaise jars by the window, each half-filled with soil—"will be your worm's motel."

"Worms check in," Kip Edwards said solemnly, "but they don't check out."

Very funny, thought Maggie. But some kids laughed.

"All right," Mr. O. said, "come on up, one table at a time, grab a jar and a paper plate, and we'll do our best to find each of you a nice, juicy worm."

"A paper plate? Are we going to eat the worms?" Kip asked. More laughter. Mr. O. grinned. He liked a lot of kidding around in his classes.

When it was Maggie and Matt's turn, Maggie hid herself behind Matt as he held out their jar to Mr. O. Since she was the shortest girl in the class—half a head shorter than Alycia—she managed to shield herself from direct contact with the worm terrarium. But she could see Mr. O. stirring through the dirt with a large wooden spoon as if he were searching for raisins in a huge bowl of bran cereal.

"Here's one for *you*," he said. With the spoon, he scooped out the worm and deposited it, wriggling, in Matt and Maggie's jar. Maggie swallowed hard. "Next!"

When everyone had a worm, Mr. O. called the class to attention with another blow on his whistle. "Okay, take your worms out of the jars and put them on the paper plates. The paper plates will be your worm observation platforms. Go ahead, watch them for a while. You can poke or prod them a bit with your pencil eraser, if you do it gently. Pay attention. See what they do."

Maggie sat frozen. So Matt reached into the jar and, to Maggie's horror, actually picked up their worm with his bare fingers. Maggie gave one involuntary shudder and stifled the urge to scream. She couldn't believe that not a foot away from her lay a loose, slimy, slithering worm that could any minute come wiggling off the plate toward her unprotected hand. She snatched her hand off the table, into the relative safety of her lap, and inched her chair a bit farther away from Matt.

"Hey, Maggie," Kip whispered piercingly from behind her. "You're not afraid of worms, are you?"

Maggie tried to ignore him. Why wasn't he asking the same thing of Alycia? Alycia was Kip's lab partner, after all, and Maggie hadn't given Kip any reason to tease her: so far she hadn't done a single, solitary thing to betray her fear. Except for one little startle. And one swallowed scream.

"Hey, Maggie, my worm is getting away!" Kip called out merrily. "It's off its plate! It's heading toward your shoulder!"

Maggie refused to respond. She hoped Kip was kidding. But she didn't want to turn around to see.

"It's coming closer, Maggie." Kip made his voice low and ominous. Maggie tried to tune him out.

"Oops, Maggie, I've lost it! Look out!"

Maggie felt something soft and limp land in her hair. She couldn't help herself: she screamed. Whenever she tried to scream in a nightmare, no sound came out. Here it did.

Someone—Matt?—reached over and plucked the *thing* out of her hair.

Finally, she made herself open her eyes. Matt, whose ears must still be hurting from the intensity of her shriek, held dangling from his hand a thick, brown, six-inch-long . . . rubber band.

"Kip, what is going on here?" Mr. O. was beside their table, his hand warm and steadying on Maggie's shoulder, real anger in his voice.

"I didn't throw a worm at her, honest I didn't. It was just a rubber band."

"Is that true, Maggie?"

Maggie was too embarrassed to answer. She could only watch as Matt dropped the offending rubber band onto Mr. O.'s outstretched palm.

"It was a *joke*," Kip said loudly. "I didn't think *anybody* would be scared of a *rubber band*."

"All right," Mr. O. said, giving Kip—and Maggie?—an uncharacteristically stern look before he headed back to his desk. "I think we've had enough introduction to our worms for today. Put your worms away and get out your notebooks."

Maggie felt her cheeks burn with shame as Matt calmly returned their worm to its jar. How could she have known it was a rubber band? Kip had tried as hard as he could to make her think it was a real live worm. Though she had to admit that most people wouldn't have screamed the way she had even for a real live worm, let alone for a real live rubber band.

Mr. O. still looked angry. Was he mad at Kip? At her? Both of them?

"Jake."

Jake Dycus had actually raised his hand to ask a question. Usually Jake showed no interest in school whatsoever. Usually he sat doodling on his desk with a sneering smile playing at the corners of his mouth.

"I was just wondering: What happens if you refuse to do the dissection?" Jake flipped back his hair as he spoke. He had an intense, interesting face, usually half-hidden by his jet-black hair, worn a lot longer than the other boys wore theirs. Maggie liked to watch him sometimes, because he was so different from everybody else in their class. Now he was the only one daring enough to ask Maggie's own unspoken question.

"Refuse?" Mr. O. asked, as if he didn't understand the word.

"What if you think dissections are immoral?"

"Anyone who does not complete a required lab assignment for any reason receives an F for that assignment." Mr. O.'s voice had an unfamiliar edge to it, perhaps left over from his irritation at the rubber-band scene. "If you receive three or more F's in the trimester, you receive an F for your final grade."

But, meeting Maggie's worried eyes, Mr. O. let his face melt into a smile, and Maggie felt a rush of grateful relief. He wasn't angry at *her*, after all.

"All right, campers." Mr. O turned to the board. "Annelida. The name is from the Latin. *Annellus* means 'little ring.' Segmented worms are made of joined segments, or rings."

Maggie picked up her pen and started taking notes, covering line after line in her notebook with her neat, small script. But although one part of her mind was paying attention to Mr. O.'s lecture, the other part was focused on Friday. Maggie didn't want to dissect a worm, and she didn't want to get an F in biology, either—not in her favorite subject, not from a teacher she loved.

How many biology students does it take not to dissect a worm? Somehow Maggie was going to have to find out.

2

"What are we going to *do*?" Maggie asked Alycia as the two girls hurried down the crowded halls of Grand Valley Middle School to lunch. She could hear her voice squeaking, the way it did when she was agitated about something.

"It's okay," Alycia said calmly. "I already figured it out."

"And?" Maggie asked, trying to make her voice low and unmouselike.

"I'm going to let Kip do it. It doesn't matter which person actually *does* it. I mean, one of us has to be the one to hold the knife, or the scalpel, or whatever it is. It might as well be Kip."

Kip would do it for Alycia, too. Maggie had a feeling he liked Alycia, or at least respected her. After all, he

13

hadn't thrown a rubber band in Alycia's hair that morning.

Alycia made it all sound logical enough. Maybe Maggie could let Matt "do" their worm. But Maggie couldn't count on Matt the way Alycia could count on Kip. Matt didn't throw rubber bands at girls, but he didn't do them favors, either. And Matt didn't even laugh at Mr. O.'s jokes. He was so stern and serious, so committed to science, ready to dissect a human corpse if one were to be laid out conveniently in front of him. Matt wasn't going to let Maggie get out of doing her fair share of the dissection.

Maggie would have to be sick on Friday. It wouldn't be too hard. She felt sick already, just thinking about it.

No. It wouldn't work. When people were sick for a lab, Mr. O. made them do a makeup lab after school the following week. Being sick didn't get you out of a lab any more than it got you out of a test. However bad it would be to dissect a worm with Matt, it would be worse doing it all by herself after school, with Mr. O. watching every move she made—or didn't make.

Maggie fought a surge of panic. She'd think of something by Friday; she had to.

What was Jake going to do? Maybe Maggie should ask him. In class that morning, he had sounded pretty opposed to dissections. But Maggie had never had a conversation with Jake, and she felt shy at the thought

14

of trying to start one, especially given how good-looking he was, in his own dark, brooding way.

When they reached the cafeteria, Maggie and Alycia claimed their favorite table, by the window and far away from the noise and confusion of the cafeteria line. They always brought their lunches from home, anyway.

Maggie made her own lunch, usually peanut butter and strawberry jam on raisin bread, with a thermos of milk and a small bag of whatever cookies were on sale at King Soopers that week. Alycia's mother made hers. Mrs. Eagen didn't work, so she had time to copy lunches out of parenting magazines. Today Alycia had a pita-bread pocket stuffed with ham and cheese chunks and shredded lettuce, with poppy-seed dressing in its own little chilled container for Alycia to add right before eating. In addition, she had cut-up vegetables, with dilled yogurt dip, and three plump, soft, homemade oatmeal raisin cookies.

Maggie liked peanut butter and jam. Still, as she looked at Alycia, pouring her poppy-seed dressing into her pita-pocket sandwich, Maggie couldn't help feeling a spasm of envy, not so much for Alycia's lunch as for the ease with which she had already figured out her escape from the worm dissection.

In English class sixth period, as Ms. Bealer droned on about the opinion essay that was due in two weeks,

Maggie let her thoughts wander back to the topic of envy. Was it wrong to be jealous of your best friend? But how could you not be jealous when your best friend had everything? For starters, Alycia had: being tall; a mother who didn't work (and who didn't make sarcastic jokes all the time); being good at sports; living in Pinewood Preserve; pierced ears (Maggie's mother considered all body piercing a form of mutilation); turning thirteen first (Maggie's birthday was still a month away); and a father. To this list, Maggie now added: great lunches; and not having to do dissections.

Who wouldn't be jealous of a friend like that? Even though Alycia never bragged about any of it and shared treats from her lunches as readily as she shared favorite books and patterns for the sewing and knitting projects that Maggie and Alycia liked to do together.

Was there anything at all that Maggie had that made *her* special? Until recently, Maggie would have had to answer no. Then, a few weeks ago, right before winter break, Maggie had had one of her long, after-school conversations with Mr. O. It was about evolution and divine creation and whether you could believe in both. Maggie had been afraid you couldn't, but Mr. O. had said you could, that scientists who believed in God only believed in Him *more* when they learned about the wonderful way in which the world had evolved. Maggie had felt so grateful to Mr. O. that day, because that was exactly how she felt about the universe.

Then, afterward, Alycia had asked her, almost crossly, "What were you guys talking about *this* time?" and Maggie had known that the relationship she had with Mr. O. was different from the relationship Alycia had with him. Mr. O. liked all the kids in the class—even, or especially, the rambunctious boys whom he kidded so much. But he liked Maggie more. Maggie only hoped that he would still like her after Friday.

Maggie was cozily curled up on the living room couch, reading ahead on the very uncozy subject of segmented worms, when she heard her mother's voice at the front door.

"Maggles! I'm home!"

Maggie's mother had an unlimited collection of pet names for Maggie, all variations on Maggie's name.

Her mother gave Maggie a quick kiss on the forehead and then flung herself down on the other end of the living room couch without even bothering to take off her coat. "This job," she said, "is turning out to be Mistake Number Three."

Mistake Number One, as Maggie knew all too well, had been marrying Maggie's father, who had walked out on them eight years ago, when Maggie was four.

Mistake Number Two had been dropping out of college after marrying him, so that her mom was still struggling to finish her B.A. while some of the other parents—Alycia's father, for one—had Ph.D.s. But Maggie's mother changed her mind with some frequency about which catastrophe in her life constituted Mistake Number Three. It could be anything from failing to drain the spinach well enough for spinach lasagna to locking her car keys in the car on a hot day while three sacks of frozen goods melted all over the upholstery.

"What happened today?" Maggie asked, closing her biology book. Her mother usually had a story to tell from work. Sometimes Maggie felt more as if she and her mother were roommates, commiserating over their lives together, than mother and daughter.

"We have twenty-two faculty members in the history department and two secretaries. But each of the twenty-two thinks Barb and I can spend a hundred percent of our time working for them. And you know who the worst is, don't you? The absolute worst? Bob Eagen. I'm supposed to drop everything else and work full-time on *his* conference. Because you and Alycia are friends, I suppose. He always asks about you right before he gives me some ridiculous, nitpicky assignment. Like, 'How's Maggie? Oh, and while we're chatting, could you call university catering and tell them that two of our speakers are vegans, not just vegetarians, and another one is allergic to shellfish, and the head table needs to have eight chairs, not seven.' "

"What's a vegan?" Maggie asked.

"Someone who doesn't eat any animal products at all. Not only meat and fish but milk, butter, eggs, cheese—even honey. Bob says this one guy won't even eat honey, because it's exploiting the bees."

Maggie's mom gave a little snort of laughter. "Try coming up with a menu for someone like that." She took off her coat, but, instead of hanging it in the closet, draped it over a chair. "How was *your* day, Mags?"

"We have to dissect a worm. On Friday. In biology."

"Oh, no!" Maggie's mother groaned sympathetically. "Yuckeroo."

Maggie could tell that her mother was waiting for the rest of the story. She wasn't sure that she could stand sharing the part about the rubber band in her hair, but when she started in on it, she found herself talking faster and faster until the whole humiliating episode had spilled out.

"That little twit," Maggie's mother said when Maggie had finished.

"I guess he thought he was being funny."

"Hardy har har," Maggie's mother said with exaggerated disdain. "See how hard I'm laughing?"

"Anyway, I'm not going to be able to do it," Maggie said. "I can't cut up a worm."

"Sure you can."

"No, I can't. Really, I can't." Although it wasn't a question of whether she *could* do it but of whether she *would*. And Maggie knew she wouldn't. It was wrong to kill something on purpose, just to cut it up to see what its insides looked like.

"Oh, Mags, you close your eyes and hold your nose and do it. Like changing a poopy diaper. Or cleaning up throw-up when it's all over the bed. It's not your favorite thing, but you do it, and you get through it, and then it's done. Unless it's throw-up, and then as soon as you put on the clean sheets and the clean pillowcases and the clean pajamas, the kid throws up all over again." Maggie's mother laughed.

"I was thinking . . ." Maggie began slowly. "If you wrote me a note? Saying you didn't want me to do it? Like that it was against our religion or something . . ."

Maggie's voice trailed off. She and her mother didn't really have a religion, not the formal kind where you went to church on Sundays. But Maggie believed in God, a God who had made every creature in every phylum they had studied so far. And Maggie knew that if she did have a religion, her own Maggie McIntosh religion, her religion would say that you weren't supposed to kill *anything* at all.

"Mags, listen. One thing I've learned over the last

eight years is that you don't get anywhere by running away from your problems, contrary to what some people may think. You're getting A's in biology, you want to keep on getting A's in biology. So you do what you have to do. I have a job, I want to keep on having a job, I do what *I* have to do." She gave Maggie a small smile. "What do you want for dinner?"

Maggie shrugged. She wasn't hungry. Thinking about the worm dissection had taken away her appetite.

"Let's stick a frozen pizza in the oven. Do you have any homework?"

"Not too much. About an hour in math. And I'm trying to do a little biology every day so the exam won't sneak up on me. And I still need to practice that new Bach piece for piano, and I have to get started on an opinion essay for English."

"An opinion essay! I wish somebody at my office would ask *me* to write an opinion essay. I have some opinions that would surprise a few of them. What are you going to write it on?"

"I don't know yet. Maybe I'll write it on—"

Maggie and her mother both said at the same time, "Dissections!"

"I know some vegans you can call if you want fuel for your fire," Maggie's mother said, reaching over to give her a hug. "I happen to know exactly where they're going to be sitting at a certain conference and exactly what their menu is going to be."

Maggie hugged her mom back. Some of her friends didn't want to hug their moms anymore, but Maggie did. Besides, she had no one else to hug. For the first three years after he'd left, Maggie's father had sent her presents on her birthday and at Christmas, but then he had married somebody else, and Maggie hadn't heard from him since, except for the child-support check that came to her mother every month, the check that he was required by law to send. Maggie's heart had raced as she looked through the mail every day before last Christmas, but there had been no card from her father, no present, no phone call: nothing.

"So is it pizza time?" her mother asked.

"Yup," Maggie said. Hungry or not, she had to keep up her strength for what was to come.

"All right," her mom said. "And then I can study for my chemistry exam, and you can spout off some opinions for English, and we can both astonish the world. If the world isn't too dumb to notice. Which it probably is. But let's astonish it anyway."

3

When Maggie made herself walk into biology class on Tuesday, at least she knew exactly what to expect: a classroom crawling with worms. And one of them—no doubt an especially agile and active one—would be hers.

Today Mr. O. had on one of his Mickey Mouse ties—not the one with lots of little Mickeys printed all over it, but the one with the huge Mickey grinning out from the widest part of the tie, giving a jaunty wave that would have made Maggie want to wave back under less wormy circumstances.

"Campers!" As usual, Mr. O. jumped right in. "How many bureaucrats does it take to change a light bulb?"

Kip knew the answer this time: "One to do it, forty-four to do the paperwork."

Mr. O. added Kip's name to the Light Bulb Hall of Fame list that he kept in one corner of the chalkboard. Maggie's name wasn't there. She had thought about checking to see if there were any light bulb joke books in the library, but had decided against it. If she knew the answers to Mr. O.'s jokes ahead of time, it would spoil the fun of hearing them in class.

Too soon, joke time was over and worm time had begun.

"All right, campers! Your worms await you!" Mr. O. announced. "Come and get 'em!"

Maggie sat completely still, wearing what she hoped was a blank stare of incomprehension: come and get *what*? So Matt was the one to retrieve their worm jar and paper plate from the low shelf under the classroom window. Maggie noticed that Kip was the one collecting the worm he shared with Alycia.

Despite his remarks on Monday, Jake was getting the worm for his table, his face showing no expression. As he turned back toward his seat, his eyes met Maggie's and held them for a long moment, as if to say that he understood why she wasn't collecting her table's worm. He really was good-looking. Maggie wondered if he ever smiled. Not that the prospect of a worm dissection was anything to smile about.

Mr. O. explained that they would be testing their worm's sensitivity to light and touch and recording their observations in their lab notebooks. *Light* didn't sound too terrible. *Touch* Maggie didn't even want to think about.

"Let's start with light," Matt said. He handed Maggie the flashlight Mr. O. had given them and crouched beside the table, at eye level with the worm.

Maggie couldn't very well refuse to shine a flashlight on the worm. That would be carrying squeamishness too far, even for her. She clicked on the flashlight and aimed the beam in the general direction of the paper plate, trying not to think about what it was shining *on*.

"Shine it on the anterior end," Matt ordered, sounding like a surgeon giving instructions to his operating-room nurse. Maggie shifted the flashlight awkwardly. She clearly wasn't cut out for O.R. duty. "No, the *other* end. Bring it in closer."

Reluctantly, Maggie moved the flashlight a couple of inches closer, careful to keep her hand still a good foot away from the worm.

With a gesture of impatience, Matt snatched the flashlight from Maggie and positioned it to suit himself. Fine! This was one job Maggie didn't mind being fired from.

But Maggie had to look at the worm at least enough to have something to write in her notebook about its reaction to light. She made herself glance down at the paper plate.

Wait. Their worm was moving toward the rim of their paper plate—the wrong rim. Under the focused beam of Matt's flashlight, it was propelling itself grotesquely off the edge of the plate, onto the table, heading unmistakably toward Maggie.

"Matt!" Maggie tried to keep her voice to an anguished mouse-squeak. "It's getting away!"

Matt didn't do anything. The worm kept advancing.

"Matt! Get it!"

Without taking his eyes off the worm, Matt replied coldly, "This is a scientific *experiment*. Our job is to *observe* worm behavior, not to *interfere* with it."

Maggie didn't scream this time, but she did scoot her chair away, until she almost bumped into the next lab table. Finally Mr. O. called out, "Okay, campers, move on to your next experiment." Matt made a careful measurement of the distance the worm had traveled toward Maggie, in centimeters. Then he deftly retrieved their worm and deposited it back on the paper plate.

Somehow Maggie survived the rest of the class. Matt did the other worm experiments unassisted. For "sensitivity to touch," he methodically poked at the writhing worm with the eraser end of his pencil, as Maggie took care to keep her own eraser worm-free. After a while, she hardly even pretended to watch. Maybe she *could* get through the dissection the same way as Alycia, after all.

"Maggie, I need to see you after class for a minute," Mr. O. called out above the scramble of people returning their worm motels to the worm shelf.

Maybe not.

"Do you have lunch now?" Mr. O. asked Maggie when the bell had rung and the others had begun streaming out of the room.

Maggie nodded.

"So do I. Why don't you grab your lunch, come get me in the teachers' room, and we'll eat back here. There're some things we need to talk about."

On her way to her locker to collect her peanut butter and jelly sandwich, Maggie didn't know if she felt more scared or excited at the thought of eating lunch with Mr. O. She had never had lunch with a teacher before; she had never been inside the teachers' room. As far as she knew, Mr. O. had never had lunch with anyone else in their class, certainly not with Alycia. But Maggie knew what Mr. O. wanted to talk about. He wanted to talk about worms.

Clutching her lunch bag tight in one hand, Maggie knocked timidly at the door of the teachers' room with the other. No one answered, so she knocked again, louder.

Ms. Bealer, Maggie's English teacher, opened the door and looked down at her suspiciously, making Maggie feel even shorter.

"Is Mr. O. here?" Maggie asked.

"Maggie! Come on in!" she heard him call.

Maggie's first glimpse of the teachers' room was a huge disappointment. It was just a regular, not very nice room, with a few ugly tables scattered about on an ugly linoleum floor. Its only special feature was that it had a mini-kitchen on one wall, with a microwave, refrigerator, and sink. But otherwise it looked like a smaller version of the school cafeteria. Maggie had always imagined the teachers' room as a posh, private club, sort of like the elegant tearoom at the Brown Palace Hotel in Denver.

Mr. O. was retrieving his lunch from the refrigerator.

"All set?" he said.

Maggie nodded. Then Mr. O. led the way back to their classroom. It was strange to think of eating lunch in a room so filled with worms, on a table where worms had been slithering a few minutes earlier. But Maggie tried not to think about it.

"Ah, peanut butter and jelly," Mr. O. said when Maggie unwrapped her soggy little sandwich. With a conspiratorial grin, he pulled out his own sandwich. "Peanut butter and jelly. Grape jelly?"

"Strawberry jam."

"But creamy peanut butter?"

Maggie smiled back at him. "Definitely."

For a moment they both munched their sandwiches

in companionable silence. Maggie would never again envy Alycia's pita-pocket sandwiches. She would be content with peanut butter and jelly for the rest of her life, savoring the knowledge that it was Mr. O.'s favorite sandwich, too.

When they had both finished their sandwiches, Mr. O. took a big swig of milk. Maggie hadn't known that teachers drank milk with lunch; she had assumed they all drank coffee. Then he said, "So, Maggie. We have to do something about you and worms."

Maggie didn't know what to say. "I just . . . hate them."

"They don't bite, you know. We're not talking about rattlesnakes here."

"I know. But they . . . *slither.*"

"Maggie." Mr. O. looked at her reproachfully, his tone saying, *Come on, Maggie, I expect more from you than that.* "You are one of the two best biology students in our class."

Even as Maggie flushed with pleasure at the praise, she wondered who the other one was. It had to be Matt.

"I don't want to see you throw away your chance to get a real education in biology. I hate to say this, Maggie, but it's important, so I will. Squeamishness about worms—it fits the cliché, the stereotype, of what our society expects of girls. A boy sees a worm, he wants to find out what makes it act the way it does. A girl sees a worm, she squeals, 'Ooh, a worm!' The result is that the boy learns something about biology, and the girl doesn't."

Maggie felt ashamed. She didn't want to be a stereotype.

"Have you ever wondered why I assigned all boy-girl lab partners last September? I've read a number of studies that report that middle-school girls who are every bit as smart as middle-school boys tend to do worse than the boys in science. I assigned boy-girl partners to try to keep that from happening, to keep the boys and girls working together. But my plan is going to backfire if the girls let the boys do the experiments for them."

Maggie had to admit that the plan certainly was backfiring this week.

"So, Maggie, what do you say? Will you try to get to know your worm? He's really not such a bad little guy."

Maggie nodded. She would have agreed to anything in the world, if Mr. O. had asked her for it in that low, earnest, caring voice.

But she couldn't help thinking: If you really got to know a worm, if you established a personal *relationship* with it, how could you turn around then and *kill* it? Wasn't there something hypocritical about getting involved with a creature that you were going to murder and cut into pieces three days later?

"Where were you?" Alycia demanded as she sat down next to Maggie in sixth-period English.

Maggie felt shy about saying it, but she didn't want to lie to Alycia. "I—well, I had lunch with Mr. O."

Alycia's eyes widened. "No kidding!"

"It wasn't any big deal," Maggie said quickly. "He just wanted to give me a pep talk about worms. You know: 'Love your worm, worms are your friends.'"

"Ugh," Alycia said. "I can't think of anything I'd rather not talk about while I'm eating." But Maggie still thought that Alycia looked jealous.

Ms. Bealer called the class to attention. She was a tall woman, even taller than Mr. O., and she never told jokes in class, light bulb or otherwise.

"Boys and girls," Ms. Bealer said. She was the only teacher who called the class "boys and girls." Mr. O. always said "campers." Other teachers said "Hey, gang," or "you guys." Ms. Kocik, Maggie's social studies teacher, her favorite teacher after Mr. O., called them "intrepid seekers after truth."

"I hope you are all beginning to work on your opinion essays. Remember, they are due in class two weeks from tomorrow. Let me review the format that I want

31

you to use in writing your essays. The first paragraph states the issue you will be considering. The particular thesis that you are defending should be stated in the last sentence of the first paragraph . . ."

Ms. Bealer kept on talking. Maggie had learned how to listen to Ms. Bealer with part of her mind while thinking her own thoughts with the rest.

On a blank piece of paper at the back of her notebook, she wrote, "Dissection—Against." She'd probably have to do some research in the library, but she could at least start out by gathering her thoughts. She began writing:

> 1. *Thou shalt not kill. Not: thou shalt not kill except to do dissections.*

So far, so good. How could anybody disagree with the Bible?

> 2. *Everything has a right to life.*

Even better. It sounded like the Declaration of Independence. How could anybody disagree with the Declaration of Independence? The only problem was that Maggie wasn't sure that this particular self-evident truth was actually true. Did *everything* have a right to life, liberty, and the pursuit of happiness? Did mosquitoes? Did bacteria? Did germs?

3. Biology is the science of life, not the science of death.

That sounded snappy, almost like a bumper sticker. Maggie could imagine wearing it on a button. Not that she ever would. Mr. O. wouldn't like it, and Maggie would never want to do anything to disappoint him. But it seemed right, nonetheless.

By the time the bell rang, Maggie had covered three pages with notes. She was going to try to do the rest of the worm experiments; she had promised Mr. O. that she would. But, promise or no promise, she wasn't going to do the worm dissection. And if that disappointed Mr. O.—well, maybe if she wrote a good enough opinion essay, he would somehow understand.

4

On afternoons when Maggie didn't have a piano lesson and Alycia didn't have basketball practice, they usually did their homework together, either at Alycia's house or at Maggie's. Maggie liked Alycia's house better, and Alycia liked Maggie's better.

Alycia's house was in the Pinewood Preserve subdivision, about half a mile from the middle school. Alycia had told Maggie that there was a rule in the subdivision that your mailbox had to be painted the same color as your house and have the same cedar shingles on its little roof. Alycia's sprawling, split-level house was gray. Her mailbox was gray. The basketball hoop next to her driveway had a gray backboard.

Maggie and her mother lived in a tiny apartment

built in a converted two-car garage in the old neighborhood right next to the university. Downstairs, they had a living room and a kitchen; upstairs, their two bedrooms and a shared bath. No dining room, no family room, no rec room, no mud room, no study, no two-story entrance hall. Not even a garage, because their apartment was already somebody else's garage. No basketball backboard, of any color.

Maggie loved Alycia's house because it was spacious and elegant, and Mrs. Eagen was always there, baking something yummy for Alycia's lunches.

"But your apartment is cozier," Alycia had told Maggie. "And I *like* that it's messy. And that your mother *isn't* there."

That day they went to Alycia's. Mrs. Eagen served them a plate of homemade gingersnaps and hot chocolate made from real milk and cocoa and sugar, not from a powdered mix.

When Alycia's mother had finally disappeared into another part of the house, Maggie said meaningfully, "Three more days."

"Three more days?" Alycia looked as if she honestly didn't know what Maggie was talking about.

"To W-day. Worm day."

"Oh, *that*. I told you, let Matt do it. That's what boys are *for*."

x

35

With Mr. O.'s lunchtime conversation still echoing in Maggie's ears, Alycia's remark sounded pretty sexist. But Maggie didn't say anything.

"Speaking of boys," Alycia went on, "I saw Jake after school yesterday, and he was smoking. It didn't look like it was his first time, either."

"That's dumb," Maggie said automatically. But as Maggie pictured Jake smoking, she imagined him, through the haze of his cigarette, staring at her wordlessly with those dark, intense eyes.

"Well, you know Jake. He has to be Mr. Cool." Alycia lowered her voice, even though no one else was listening. "I heard his dad left."

"Left?" Maggie felt her throat tightening.

"Just took off. Kip told me. So maybe that's why—" Alycia broke off. "I didn't mean—"

"I know," Maggie said. She could have finished Alycia's sentence for her: I didn't mean that everybody whose father leaves is a budding juvenile delinquent.

Lots of kids at school had divorced parents. It was hardly a big deal. Unless you were the one whose parents were divorced. Then it was a big deal, at least to you. And it felt strange to think of people, other kids, saying to each other about *her*, Maggie, "I heard her dad left." It was strange to think of the biggest, saddest fact about your life being a piece of gossip told by one kid to another, over hot chocolate and gingersnaps, in somebody's country-style kitchen.

"What are you writing your opinion essay on?" Alycia asked Maggie, obviously to change the subject.

"Guess."

"Why knitting is more fun than crocheting."

Maggie whacked Alycia with her gingham napkin. "Dissections. And why they're not fun at all, at least for whoever gets dissected."

Alycia looked impressed. "You picked a hard one. I'm doing mine on recycling. Well, really on precycling, they call it. How people shouldn't buy stuff that has too much packaging. Like those individually wrapped slices of cheese. Or juice boxes. And they *shouldn't*. I feel like stopping people in line at King Soopers and saying, 'Don't buy that!' "

Alycia took another small bite of her gingersnap. She always nibbled around the edges of a cookie, like a mouse. Maggie sometimes squeaked like a mouse; Alycia ate like a mouse. It was plainly a sign that they were meant to be best friends. Plus, they were both perfectly happy to sit for hours, knitting afghan squares or figuring out how to make woven bracelets from a craft kit or working a complicated pattern in counted cross-stitch.

"Well, I don't think people should do dissections," Maggie said. It was far worse to kill another living creature than it was to buy individually wrapped cheese slices.

"Lucky for me that boys aren't people," Alycia said. She laughed, and Maggie smiled. Maggie couldn't help appreciating the way that Alycia was always in control where boys were concerned; it was amusing to watch hapless males like Kip scurrying to do her bidding. But boys *were* people, and if dissection was wrong, it was just as wrong whether you did it yourself or made your lab partner do it for you.

"Should we get started?" Maggie asked, a bit too abruptly.

"Sure," Alycia said, pushing the plate of gingersnaps aside to make room for their books. When Maggie and Alycia studied together, they really studied. Both girls liked to do well academically, even though some of their other friends thought it was dumb to care about school. It was another main thing Maggie and Alycia had in common. They had done homework together for so many years that Alycia's round handwriting was as familiar to Maggie as her own.

Maggie opened her English notebook and read over her notes for her dissection paper. Then she picked up her pen and began writing.

In biology class on Wednesday, Maggie decided to force herself to get over her fear of worms. When Matt set the worm motel on their lab table, Maggie didn't let herself shrink away in her usual horror. Instead she looked at the worm, calmly and carefully. It really wasn't very terrifying, at least not when safely contained in the mayonnaise jar.

Maggie felt Mr. O.'s eyes on her.

"I think—I want to touch it," Maggie said to Matt.

"Be my guest." Matt pushed the jar closer to Maggie.

Now what? Maggie thought that she could stand touching their worm with the tip of one finger if Matt took it out of the jar and put it on the paper plate, but she didn't think she could pick it up, just like that.

"Would you put it on the plate for me?" Maggie asked meekly. She was sure Alycia didn't sound so humble and apologetic when she got Kip to do things for her.

Matt looked disgusted, but he obliged. On the plate, the worm stretched, as if relieved to be out of the cramped quarters of its glass prison.

It was now or never. Maggie readied her right index finger. She brought it within three inches of the worm before she lost her nerve. She thought of Mr. O. again. *Will you try to get to know your worm? He's really not such a bad little guy.* She had to do it. She couldn't disappoint Mr. O.

Maggie touched the worm.

Her heart racing with exhilaration now, not terror, she looked up at Mr. O. He gave her an approving grin.

She touched the worm again and felt a fierce kind of triumph surge through her. There was nothing in the world, she suddenly knew, nothing at all, as powerful as facing a fear and overcoming it. Right then, in that moment, Maggie felt she could touch a hundred worms. She could touch a hundred *snakes.*

She turned to Matt, wanting to share this moment with *someone,* even with him. To her surprise, he was smiling, too. His was a superior, condescending smile, not like Mr. O.'s grin of congratulation, but it was definitely a smile.

"You want to put it back, or should I?" Matt asked then.

Maggie didn't hesitate. "I'll do it. I just pick him up? Like by the middle?"

"That's all there is to it."

Maggie reached down, with thumb and forefinger this time. She grasped the worm around the middle, firmly enough so that he couldn't wriggle away, but not so firmly that she squished him. There! She dropped him back in the jar. He *wasn't* such a bad little guy.

"Let's give him a name," Maggie suggested. "What's a good name for a worm? How about Squirmy?"

"You don't name worms." Matt looked disgusted again. Their brief moment of camaraderie was apparently over. "It's not a pet. It's not even going to be *alive* two days from now. We're *dissecting* it Friday, remember?"

Unbelievably, Maggie had, for a few moments, forgotten.

"Not me," Maggie said. "Maybe you, but not me."

"Are you going to keep up this squeamish stuff all year?"

"I'm not squeamish." Well, as of five minutes ago, she wasn't. "I touched him. You saw me. I just think it's wrong to dissect animals, that's all."

Matt snorted with annoyance. "Come on, you eat animals, don't you?"

"That's not the same thing."

"Why not? You kill animals to eat them, you kill animals to dissect them. Either way, they're dead. What's the difference?"

"*I* don't kill animals to eat them. *I've* never killed any cows or pigs." Besides, though Maggie didn't say it out loud, it was hard to think of hamburger as really having come from a cow, or bacon as really having come from a pig.

"So you have someone else do your killing for you. *That's* admirable. I'm sure the cows and pigs are appreciative. 'We're getting slaughtered, but Maggie McIntosh didn't do it. She's only going to *eat* me, she's not going to *kill* me.' "

Maggie tried to think back to the arguments she was

41

working on for her dissection essay. *Thou shalt not kill. Everything has a right to life.* Matt was right. Even if she wasn't killing cows and pigs and sheep and chickens, somebody was. And if everything had a right to life, cows and pigs and sheep and chickens did, too.

But still . . .

"Wait a minute," Maggie said. "*You* aren't a vegetarian. Why are you trying to make *me* feel guilty about eating meat?" She had Matt there.

"I'm *not* a vegetarian," Matt agreed calmly. "I'm also not claiming that dissections are immoral."

"But *eating* meat—I mean, people have to eat. They don't have to do dissections."

"Did you ever hear of tofu? Or peanut butter? Or vegetables? There're plenty of other things to eat."

"It's different to kill something just to see what it looks like inside," Maggie insisted. "To kill something out of *curiosity*."

"It's called *science*," Matt said. "It's probably the reason you're alive today, instead of dead from smallpox, or TB, or a strep infection."

"All right, campers." Mr. O., who had been helping some kids in the back of the room, was standing next to their lab table. "What seems to be the problem here?"

"Nothing," Maggie said, hoping Mr. O. hadn't overheard their conversation. She wanted to have her thoughts all worked out before she explained to him—

tried to explain to him—why she wouldn't be doing the dissection on Friday.

"We were having a philosophical discussion," Matt said loftily.

"I touched my worm again," Maggie said, wondering if Mr. O. would give her another approving smile. He did, and Maggie once more basked in the glow of his good opinion. Then he moved on to another lab table.

It had been a momentous morning, all right.

Maggie had touched a worm.

And she had become a vegetarian.

5

Maggie wasn't sure how to tell her mother that she wasn't eating meat anymore. In one way, it shouldn't matter. Maggie could hardly remember the last time her mother had gone to the trouble to cook a real meal—the kind where you plan a menu, and shop for groceries, and use a recipe. Usually the two of them foraged in the fridge together like roommates. But Maggie still felt uneasy. Her mother didn't seem to like those vegetarians at the university very much. What would she say now that her own daughter had become one?

At least her mother seemed to be in a good mood that evening. "Guess who got an A on the chemistry exam?" she warbled as she burst into the living room. "Ninety-six out of a hundred!"

"That's great, Mom," Maggie said. It was funny watching her mother's agony and ecstasy over her grades. She cared about her own grade point average even more than Maggie and Alycia cared about theirs. It was as if every A she got at college were proving something, retroactively, to Maggie's father.

"Celebrate! Celebrate!" Her mother was dancing around the living room, looking more like a crazy older sister than a thirty-four-year-old mom. Maggie couldn't imagine Alycia's mother dancing like that, with her coat still on and her shoes kicked off and her long hair flying.

At last her mother dropped down beside Maggie on the couch. "Seriously," she said, "we *should* celebrate. He only gave seven A's. How much homework do you have? Want to go out for dinner?"

"Sure." In a restaurant, Maggie could order whatever she wanted. All restaurants had some vegetarian food.

But an hour later, when Maggie studied the menu in their favorite Thai restaurant, her uneasiness returned. What would her mother say when she ordered curried tofu and eggplant? Or vegetarian delight? She always ordered beef with ginger and mushrooms. And she always shared her mother's chicken in peanut sauce.

"What looks good to you, Maggiola? Should we stick with twenty-four and thirty-seven?" They had ordered the same entrées so often that they had memorized their numbers from the menu.

"I might try something different," Maggie said off-handedly. "Maybe forty-eight."

Her mother checked her menu. "Curried *tofu*? And eggplant? You don't like tofu, remember? Tofu, the food without texture?"

"Well, fifty-one, then."

"Vegetarian delight? I hate to tell you, but that has *vegetables* in it."

In deciding so suddenly that morning to become a vegetarian, Maggie had overlooked the small fact that she disliked almost all vegetables.

"Well, you see," Maggie said uncomfortably, "I've sort of—pretty much—decided to be a vegetarian."

"What?" her mother said, although Maggie knew she had heard her the first time.

Maggie did her best to explain. Her mother replied with the same arguments Maggie had tried to use against Matt. "But, Maggles, everybody has to *eat*."

"I can eat tofu." She'd get used to those bland, deathly white, Jell-O–like, quivering squares.

"Tofu isn't *food*," her mother said. "How about fish? Do vegetarians eat fish? The curried shrimp here is extra-yummy."

Did vegetarians eat fish? Maggie had been one for

only seven hours, so she was hardly an expert on vegetarianism. She found herself wondering what Matt would say. The answer wasn't too hard to figure out. Matt would say that if she wouldn't kill a worm, she shouldn't kill a shrimp.

"No," Maggie said, twisting her napkin miserably in her lap.

"But promise me—you're not going to be a vegan, are you?"

Maggie didn't *think* she was going to be a vegan, but she couldn't remember exactly what they did and didn't eat.

"No dairy products? No milk, cheese, butter, eggs? No honey, because it exploits the bees?"

"I'm not a vegan." You didn't have to kill a cow to get milk. Maggie wasn't opposed to exploitation, just to murder.

The waitress came for their order.

"Number twenty-four. Chicken in peanut sauce. Mags?"

"Number forty-eight," Maggie said firmly. "Curried tofu and eggplant."

It wasn't too bad, actually. The curry gave the tofu some flavor, and the eggplant was cooked so much that it was barely recognizable as a vegetable. Maggie had survived her first real meal as a vegetarian. (The peanut butter and jelly sandwich she had eaten for lunch didn't count.) But it was depressing to think how many more meals she had to go. Three meals a day for—eighty?—more years. That added up to a lot of tofu.

Thursday night, Maggie had trouble sleeping. At one o'clock in the morning, she was still wide awake, staring up at the low ceiling that sloped in over her old-fashioned wooden bed.

She didn't have to worry anymore about deciding what to do. She wasn't going to do the dissection, and she wasn't going to pretend to do it by letting Matt do it for her. She'd get an F on the lab, but she could accept that—although Maggie wanted an A in biology as much as her mother wanted an A in chemistry. Still, Maggie knew that grades weren't the most important thing in the world. She wouldn't cheat for a grade. She wouldn't kill—even a worm—for a grade.

More than her grade, Maggie was lying awake worrying about Mr. O.'s reaction to her grade. How would he look when she told him she wasn't going to dissect her worm? What would he say? Could Maggie make him understand? What if she couldn't?

Maggie somehow expected the atmosphere in biology class on Friday to be somber, sorrowful. She almost thought she'd see the worm motels draped in black crepe paper and hear Chopin's funeral march playing softly on Mr. O.'s portable CD player.

Instead, Mr. O. was, if anything, more jovial and high-spirited than ever.

"Campers! How many worms does it take to change a light bulb?"

"Dead or alive?" someone called out. Maggie stiffened. Whatever killing worms was, it wasn't funny.

"One," Mr. O. answered, ignoring the question. "But it has to be a glowworm."

The class groaned appreciatively. Maggie forced a smile. It was an appropriate joke for worm dissection day. Or would have been if any jokes could be appropriate under such gruesome circumstances.

The class did fall unusually quiet as Mr. O. explained the procedure for killing the worm, by putting a small, poison-soaked cotton ball beside it in the jar. The fumes would kill it almost instantly.

This is wrong, Maggie's own voice repeated over and over again in her head. *This is wrong.*

Matt brought their worm motel to their table. *For the last time.* Maggie looked at their worm, curled up in a semicircle, so small and helpless and trusting. He probably thought they were going to take him out of his jar and put him on the paper plate again, for another hour of playtime—and freedom. But the same people who had treated him so tenderly all week and had studied him so closely—these same people were now going to *kill* him.

If Maggie had been braver, she would have snatched the jar off the table and dashed outside with it. She could have found a safe, sheltered bit of grass and dirt, and set her worm free. Instead, she sat motionless, wondering how guilty you were if you sat and did nothing while others killed. But even if she saved one worm, she couldn't save them all.

Maggie would never have believed, on Monday, that by Friday she would be crying over the death of a worm. But she was. She could feel her eyes fill to over-flowing. Their worm had done *nothing*. All he asked of life was food and water and warm, moist soil. In five minutes he would be dead.

Matt caught sight of Maggie's face. "Give me a break," he said.

"I don't want him to be dead." Maggie forced the words out in a choked whisper.

"It's a worm! It'll hardly even *notice* being dead. Worms don't think, Maggie. They barely feel."

"How do you know they don't?"

"Because they barely have a *brain*! When we dissect it, you'll see—there's next-to-nothing upstairs for them to think or feel *with*."

Maggie felt Mr. O.'s hand on her shoulder.

"Maggie." His voice was so kind and gentle that

Maggie's tears only flowed more freely. He didn't hate her—yet.

"I can't kill him." No, it was more than that, and she had to say it. "I won't kill him."

Mr. O. sighed. "Okay, Maggie." He still didn't sound mad, but he did sound disappointed. "We'll have to talk about this later. For now, I'll write you a pass, and you can spend the rest of the lab in the library."

Maggie didn't linger to say a final farewell to their worm. She grabbed her book and backpack and stumbled toward the door, feeling Alycia's sympathetic eyes upon her. But Alycia shouldn't be pitying Maggie right now; she should be joining her. Relief at escaping the horror to come mingled with anger at the shame that was being inflicted on her alone. Maggie had been dismissed: the girl who was first too squeamish to touch a worm and then too squeamish to kill one. But it wasn't a question of squeamishness. It was a simple question of right and wrong. Why couldn't anyone else see that, too?

Maggie turned back before she reached the door.

"This is wrong!" Her voice came out too loudly. She was almost shouting: "Killing is wrong!"

"Maggie, I asked you to leave." She could hear the anger in Mr. O.'s voice now—anger she had heard only once or twice before, directed at Jake, never at her.

"Maggie's right." Someone was defending her. With

Mr. O.'s stern gaze upon her, she didn't look to see who it was. She couldn't bear another minute of his cold, barely controlled wrath. She fled the room, overcome by the same sense of finality as when she had found out, so many years ago, that her father was gone forever.

6

Maggie heard footsteps in the hall behind her. For a fleeting moment she hoped it was Alycia, hurrying to tell her, "Dissecting animals *is* wrong. I'm refusing to do it, too." But she knew it wasn't.

"Hey, Maggie." Jake fell into step next to her. So it had been Jake's voice she had heard as she was leaving. It all felt oddly right. Although they had never officially spoken to each other, the way Jake had looked at her in class the other day had felt like a wordless conversation, echoing the question about dissections he had asked Mr. O. the very first day. Now he had walked out of the lab to join Maggie, making him the only person in the whole class to take her side.

"That was cool," Jake told her. "Standing up to Mr. O. like that. That took guts."

Even with Jake walking beside her, Maggie didn't feel very gutsy right now. "I didn't mean to make him mad," she said. "I just wanted—well, I *do* think it's wrong to kill animals. I just wanted to say it."

"Are you a vegetarian?" Jake asked as they kept on walking. Maggie felt a heightened consciousness of his presence beside her. She knew they made an odd pair: the bad boy and the good girl, he wearing the black leather jacket he wore every day, she wearing a corduroy jumper and blouse; his dark hair falling insolently over one eye, her blond hair held back from her face with a perky barrette. But they alone had opposed the dissection. They had that bond between them.

"Uh-huh," Maggie replied. She didn't say that she had been a vegetarian only since Wednesday. She felt shy with Jake, even shyer than she did with Matt. Both boys were cynical and contemptuous, but about different things, in different ways.

"Cool," Jake said again. Maggie savored his approval. At least *someone* approved of her choices.

"Are you?" she asked.

"I've been thinking about it. One step at a time, I guess. Walking out on that creep today, that's the first step."

"Mr. O.'s not a creep!" Even though Jake had taken her side, she couldn't let him put down Mr. O.

"Sorry," Jake said. "I forgot that you're the pet." Now he sounded more like his usual hostile self.

"He's not a creep," Maggie repeated. And she was no longer the pet. "He's the best teacher I've ever had."

"Guys like that bore me," Jake said. "They act like they're so cool and friendly, with the ties and the jokes and everything, while all the time they're waiting to nail you the minute you cross their dumb line. Authority trips bore me."

Maggie didn't say anything, so Jake went on, "My dad was like that."

Maggie noticed that he used the past tense: My dad *was* like that. So it was true that his dad had left.

"He split," Jake said then.

"That's too bad." It sounded trite, but Maggie didn't know what else to say. Should she tell him that her dad had left, too? It wasn't the kind of thing Maggie told people. It had been hard for her even to tell Mr. O.

"Oh, I'm really crying," Jake said. "See how hard I'm crying?"

They reached the library. Maggie suddenly remembered that she had left biology without her pass.

As if reading her thoughts, Jake whipped out two passes with a flourish. "I got yours when I got mine." He handed it to Maggie as if it were a thirty-dollar

55

ticket to a rock concert, and she were his date. The gesture made Maggie feel even more drawn to Jake, even though he was completely wrong about Mr. O.

Jake opened the door to the library and held it open for Maggie with an exaggerated show of gallantry. Maggie couldn't help smiling at him. And surly, sullen Jake smiled back.

"Are you okay?" Alycia asked when Maggie took her usual seat at lunch.

The concern in her voice irritated Maggie. "Sure," Maggie said. "Are *you*?" Alycia was the one with a worm's blood on her hands. If you could call it blood. Maggie called it *goo*. And of course Maggie knew that Alycia had been careful not to get worm goo on *her* hands. But she shared responsibility for the death of a worm. Maggie knew the answer now to the question she had asked an hour ago: You *are* guilty if you sit by and do nothing while others kill.

If Alycia heard the edge to Maggie's question, she chose to ignore it. "It wasn't too bad," she said. "As worm dissections go. I thought I wouldn't be able to look at it at all, but after a while I got used to it, and then it was really kind of interesting."

Alycia's words struck Maggie as chilling. It was terrible to think of all the killing that human beings had gotten used to in the history of the world. And how could the brutal murder of a worm be *interesting*?

Maggie didn't want to ask the next question, but she couldn't stop herself. "How mad was Mr. O. after Jake and I left?"

"He wasn't mad at all. He turned to the rest of the class and said, 'Anyone else for an F?' And when there was no one else, he was his regular self again, kidding with the boys, *you* know."

Maggie hadn't wanted Mr. O. to stay angry, and yet it bothered her that he had been able to move on to business as usual so quickly.

The F that Maggie had gotten, that Alycia *hadn't* gotten, was beginning to rankle, too. Maybe it was easier to get used to killing if it kept your grade point average high.

"You don't think there's anything *wrong* with dissections?" Maggie asked, her voice sliding up into squeaking range. She had unwrapped her peanut butter and jelly sandwich, but she was still too upset to eat it. She noticed that Alycia wasn't having any trouble eating her ham and cheese croissant. The pink gleam of the ham in Alycia's sandwich suddenly looked very pig-like to Maggie, very much like a sliver of flesh.

"I guess not," Alycia said. She took another ladylike

bite of pig flesh. "I mean, *I* don't want to dissect anything, but I wouldn't judge anyone else for doing it. I
don't know. Maybe it's wrong, but it's not *wrong* wrong.
I mean, it's part of biology class. Mr. O. wouldn't have
us do it if it was *really* wrong."

A week before, Maggie would have said the same
thing. She couldn't say it now.

In English, Ms. Bealer began class with an announcement. She and the other seventh-grade English teachers
had gathered together to organize a contest for the best
opinion essays. There would be a first, second, and
third prize, plus three honorable mentions. All six winning essays would be published in the middle-school
newspaper, *The Grand Valley Gazette.*

Maggie and Alycia exchanged hopeful glances.
They were the two best writers in the class, in their
own modest, unbiased opinion. With six prizes to be
awarded, they had a good chance of winning one
each.

"All essays submitted in time—remember, they are
due Wednesday, January 21—will be eligible for the
contest," Ms. Bealer said. "The important thing is not
what you argue for, but *how well* you argue for it. That
means thinking hard about what can be said for the
other side. We'll be judging your essays in part on how

successfully you respond to the best objections that can be raised to your own opinion."

That was where Maggie had an advantage over Alycia. The trouble with the precycling topic was that there was nothing to be said on the other side. What could anybody say against precycling? That garbage dumps were actually kind of attractive, in their own special way? But Maggie knew that there was plenty that could be said in favor of dissections. All she would have to do for that part of her essay was spend another five minutes listening to Matt.

What would Mr. O. do if her dissection essay won a prize and got published in the school paper for all to see? It couldn't make him much madder than he was already. Maybe when he read it—with FIRST PRIZE WIN-NER printed at the top—he'd understand why Maggie had to do what she had done today.

If Maggie could make Mr. O. understand, she'd deserve that prize.

If Maggie could make Mr. O. understand, she wouldn't need any other prize.

Maggie had trouble sleeping again that night. For some reason, her thoughts kept focusing on her father. She could hardly remember him, what he had looked like, how he had acted, the sound of his voice. When she did have a memory of him, she wasn't sure if it was a real memory or something she had mixed up, or made up, or taken from a book. She was only four when he left. Four was a long time ago.

The clock next to her bed read 3:15. Maggie switched on the light. She slipped out of the covers and, shivering in the chilly room, dug out a red-plaid shoe box she kept hidden at the back of her closet. One small shoe box—size 2½—contained everything she had left from her father.

Back in bed again, she lifted off the lid. She knew the contents of the box by heart, but she still needed to look at them every few months.

Three birthday cards, three Christmas cards, from the first three years after he had left. Maggie read the six signatures: "Love, Daddy," printed carefully in big letters, because she hadn't been able to read cursive then. One of the birthday cards said, "I miss my little girl." Another said, "I love you, honey." The other cards had no special comments at all.

A picture of the two of them together building a snowman. A picture of them carving a pumpkin. Maggie's mother had told her there were so few pictures of Maggie's father because he had been the one taking all the pictures of everybody else, but Maggie knew that her mother had thrown most of the pictures away. Once, a few years ago, her mother had ripped up all their wedding pictures. She hadn't merely thrown them in the trash; she had yanked them off the adhesive pages of the photo album and ripped them into pieces. Maggie had rescued one of them and taped it together.

She studied it now. Her father had his arm around her mother, turning her toward the camera as if to tell the world, "Look at the beautiful girl I married." Her mother was laughing, not the mocking laugh Maggie knew so well, but a laugh of pure wonder and delight.

What had happened? How could two people love each other that much and then five years later not love each other at all?

The only thing left in the box now was a picture of a bird that her father had drawn for her on the back of a grocery list, with her clumsy, four-year-old attempt to copy it. Her scribbled ball of a bird, with its two stick-like legs poking out, always brought tears to Maggie's eyes, not for herself now, but for the little girl she had been.

That was it. That was all that remained in Maggie's life of the man who was her father: six cards, two snapshots, one taped-together wedding picture, two bird drawings on scrap paper. Maggie replaced the lid and pushed the box back under her bed. Then she switched off the light and burrowed under her covers.

Where was he now? Did he ever think of her, the little girl he had left behind forever? Did he have his own little box of mementos hidden at the back of *his* closet? Or was she as forgotten as . . . a worm left shriveled on the sidewalk after the rain?

7

All weekend long, Maggie dreaded the moment Monday morning when she would have to walk in to biology class and face Mr. O. But as she slipped into her first-row seat right before the bell rang, he gave her his usual smile. Or *a* smile. Was it the same smile he gave everybody, or was it the special smile Maggie had always felt he saved for her?

This is ridiculous, Maggie told herself. She shouldn't be analyzing Mr. O.'s smiles on a scale of 1 to 10. She should be glad he had smiled at her at all.

Maggie looked toward the window. The worm motels were gone, their inhabitants all dead, murdered, including Squirmy. Maggie wondered what had become of their remains. Tossed into the trash, she supposed.

Only little children held funerals for dead worms and birds and goldfish.

"Campers!" Mr. O. blew his whistle. Maggie bet Jake hated that whistle. If "authority trips" bored him, probably whistles did, too. "How many librarians does it take to change a light bulb?"

Maggie had heard that one before. She struggled to think of the answer. She had it! She raised her hand, practically waving it the way first graders did.

"Maggie?"

"I don't know, but I can look it up for you," Maggie said, feeling a bit silly over her pride at getting it right.

Mr. O. flashed her a grin—this time Maggie was sure it was the special smile—and added her name to the Light Bulb Hall of Fame on the chalkboard. Maybe Maggie *would* look for a light bulb joke book in the library. For every dissection she didn't do, she could have a light bulb punch line to offer in compensation.

Worms were over, Mr. O. announced. They were now turning their attention to fish.

"Will we dissect a fish?" Kip asked right away.

"Next week," Mr. O. promised. "But we won't have them here in class to observe. We'll be dissecting perch, and I don't think our mayonnaise jars would make very comfortable perch motels. So I'll have the perch delivered here a week from Friday, ready to go."

Ready to go meant *already dead.*

As Mr. O. turned to the chalkboard to begin writing fish information, Matt asked Maggie, in a low scornful voice, "I suppose you think it's wrong to dissect fish, too?"

Obviously warming to his topic, he went on, "You'd take a fish home from the fish market to cook it and eat it, but not to dissect it and actually learn something about it."

Maggie welcomed Matt's sarcasm. "For your information, I no longer eat fish. Or animals."

Matt looked puzzled.

"I've become a vegetarian." *So there, Mr. Matt Dixon!*

"Since when?" Matt sounded suspicious.

"Well, since Wednesday." It didn't sound very long, but Maggie was already getting tired of peanut butter and jelly sandwiches and grilled cheese sandwiches and hard-boiled eggs. She was going to have to expand her collection of vegetarian recipes.

Maggie expected Matt to say something withering. To her surprise, he looked almost impressed. "At least you're being consistent," he said. "Consistently wrong, but consistent."

Mr. O. turned back to the class. Conversation time was over. But now Maggie actually wanted to talk more to Matt about dissections. Every argument he offered in favor of dissections was more material for her prize-winning essay.

Luckily, that afternoon Ms. Bealer gave them class

time to work on their essays in the library. Maggie sat down at Matt's table. "Can I ask you a couple of questions?" The librarian didn't mind if they talked quietly.

"Questions?" Matt asked.

"About why you believe in dissections. For my opinion essay. It's on dissection, and I want to put in the other side."

"So I'm the other side?" Matt looked pleased by his role. "Be my guest."

"Question number one. Do you think it's wrong to kill people?"

"Sure," Matt answered without hesitation. "Most of the time. Not all the time. Like, you could kill someone in self-defense. Or in a war. But most of the time, yeah, it's wrong to kill people."

"Question number two. If it's wrong to kill people, why isn't it wrong to kill animals?"

Maggie was glad to see that Matt had to think for a minute. She used the time to press on. "You don't eat people, right? Or kill people just to dissect them? Why should you treat animals differently?"

"Animals *aren't* people. That's why we treat them differently. Animals don't think. I told you, a worm barely has a brain. It has nothing to think *with*. It has nothing to think *about*."

"Worms can feel, though," Maggie said. "Squirmy didn't like it when we shone the flashlight on him. He tried to slither away." Maggie remembered the episode all too well.

"Stimulus/response. You do something, they do something. Squirmy"—Matt made a face at the name—"didn't say to himself, 'Oh, someone is shining a light on me, so I had better change direction and remove myself from this unpleasant brightness in my field of vision.' He just reacted. The way a flower turns to the sun. Animals react to things."

"Dogs and cats think," Maggie said.

"I thought we were talking about worms. If I remember correctly, you didn't walk out of a *dog* dissection."

"Cows and pigs think, and we kill them. I read somewhere that pigs are one of the most intelligent animals. Pigs think."

"Think about what?" Matt asked. "A warm bucket of slop. A roll in the mud. They're not thinking about the theory of relativity."

"Well, most people don't, either. I've never thought about the theory of relativity in my whole entire life." Maggie wasn't sure what the theory of relativity was, except that Einstein had thought it up, and it had something to do with physics, and you didn't have to dissect anything in a physics class.

Matt gave her a look as if to say, *It figures.*

"Just because a pig doesn't have great thoughts doesn't mean he doesn't think," Maggie persisted. "Or feel. A pig may not know about relativity, but he knows he doesn't want to be killed and eaten."

"A pig doesn't know anything. He doesn't even know he's a pig. You've been reading too much *Charlotte's Web*. You think every pig is Wilbur. I'm telling you, Wilbur is *fiction*. As in: made-up. As in: a character in a storybook."

Maggie knew that Matt was trying to make her concern for animals sound childish, but she wasn't going to give in. "If you stick a knife into a pig, he feels it. You can call it stimulus/whatever, but he wouldn't respond if he didn't feel something."

"Okay, animals feel pain. Maybe worms feel pain, I don't know. I'm not saying we shouldn't care about hurting animals. But any halfway decent butcher can kill an animal one, two, three. The animal doesn't even know what's happening. Do you think Squirmy knew he was being killed? *Oh, no, here comes the poisonous cotton ball!* Get real. One minute he's alive, the next he's dead. He didn't know anything. Besides, when people do dissections, it's for a reason, it's to learn something. I'm not saying people should kill animals for fun."

"So you think hunting is wrong?" Maggie asked quickly.

"I didn't say that. Hunting has a purpose, too. It keeps animal populations under control. It's part of the balance of nature. Look, don't get me started on hunting. Human beings are predators. That's what nature made us. That's what we *are*. And predators hunt prey. That's different from killing animals just to kill them— like stepping on a worm for the fun of squashing it."

"You wouldn't step on a worm?" Maggie felt as if she were on the brink of some kind of victory. She felt as if she were moving in for the kill, if vegetarians were entitled to use that metaphor.

"Just to step on one? No. Because there's no *point* to it. But did it bother me to dissect Squirmy? No. Because it was for the sake of science."

"You really think it advanced science for you to kill Squirmy?" It certainly hadn't advanced science for Kip Edwards to dissect his worm. It had probably set science back.

Matt held his ground. "I do. Maybe none of us made any discoveries about worms that are going to win us the Nobel Prize in biology, but *I* learned something about worms I couldn't have learned in any other way."

"Like what?" Maggie honestly couldn't imagine what you could learn from cutting up a worm that you couldn't learn from seeing a picture of the inside of a worm.

"Like what a worm is really like inside. Would you

want to be operated on by a surgeon who had never looked inside a real person, but only sat in front of a computer screen looking at *simulations* of surgery? I wouldn't."

"But seeing what something's really like doesn't seem important enough to kill it for."

"It's important enough to kill a *worm* for."

"Matt! Maggie!" Ms. Bealer called to them. "We didn't come to the library so that you could talk about your essays. We came here so that you could do research on them."

Matt rolled his eyes at Maggie, as if he knew that there was no better research than talking to him. Maggie found that her pulse was racing and her cheeks were flushed from the intensity of their debate. Who had won—she or Matt? No one's mind had changed, but at least Matt had admitted that people shouldn't cause pain to animals, or kill them for no good reason.

Maggie still felt there was something important she hadn't said, something that would have convinced Matt that *thinking* wasn't what mattered. So what if Squirmy couldn't read or write or do advanced physics? There were people who couldn't do those things, either. There were people who didn't know they were people, the way pigs didn't know they were pigs. Like little babies, or people who were in comas, or senile, or really handicapped. It would still be wrong to kill them. Even if they couldn't think, they were alive. What mattered—for people, for dogs, for pigs, for worms—was *living*.

When Maggie and Alycia walked out of school together after eighth period, Maggie saw Jake hanging around by the front steps, an unlit cigarette dangling from his hand. Students weren't allowed to smoke on school property, but apparently it was okay to hold a cigarette that was just being used as a prop to show how cool you were.

"Hey, Maggie," he said, giving her a slow, crooked smile. Although it was beginning to snow, he was bareheaded and his jacket was draped carelessly over one shoulder.

"You're going to catch a cold," Maggie told him in what she hoped was a playful-scolding tone, not a nagging-scolding tone. He looked even better with his jacket off than with his jacket on.

"Nah," he said. "You don't catch cold from the cold, you catch cold from germs."

Alycia pulled Maggie away before she had a chance to do more than smile in reply. "What are you talking to him for?" Alycia asked once they were out of hearing.

"I didn't talk to him, he talked to me."

"You talked back."

"So? What's wrong with Jake?"

"What *isn't* wrong? A, he smokes. B, he doesn't do any work in any of his classes. I bet he's failing everything. C, he needs a haircut. D, he thinks he's so cool. Should I go on?"

"I *like* his hair," Maggie said defiantly. It was so jet black and soft-looking as it fell down over his dark eyes.

"You don't."

"Yes, I do. I like *him*."

"Maggie! Not *like* like."

"No, not *like* like. But . . ." Maggie let the sentence trail off. Jake had stood up for her on worm day, which was more than anyone else in class had done—including Alycia, her supposed best friend. And it couldn't be easy for Jake, losing his father, however tough he tried to talk. What could Alycia know about that? And then there was Jake's hair, and the defiant thrust of his chin, and the way his face changed when he smiled.

"I just like him, that's all." They had reached Alycia's mother's car. Mrs. Eagen always came to pick up Alycia on snowy or rainy or windy afternoons.

Right then Maggie liked everything and everybody: the low sky; the thickening flakes; the thought of working on her essay some more over steaming mugs of hot chocolate at Alycia's house; the memory of Mr. O.'s forgiving smile; the thrill of her debate with Matt; the sense that Jake had been glad to see her, that he would have talked more if Alycia hadn't pulled her away, the sense that, different as they were, he liked her—really liked her, *liked* her liked her—too.

8

On worm day, Mr. O. had said to Maggie that they needed to talk "later" about her refusal to dissect, but as the following week went by, "later" never came. Mr. O. continued to smile at Maggie, and Maggie continued to smile back, but neither one initiated a conversation about dissections. By the end of the week, Maggie had almost forgotten the flash of icy anger in Mr. O.'s eyes. The next dissection was still a whole week away. And when fish day came, Mr. O. could hardly be any angrier with Maggie than he had been on worm day.

To Maggie's surprise, Matt sought her out at lunch on Friday. Alycia was home sick that day, and the other girls hadn't come to the table yet.

"I have a question for *you*," Matt said, settling himself into the chair next to hers with his hot-lunch tray. Maggie glanced disdainfully at his food. Beefaroni. Cowaroni.

"What is it?" Maggie asked. "Am I the other side for *your* opinion essay?" She was joking; she knew that Matt was writing on human genetic research, and she had no opinions about human genetic research whatsoever. Except that she wouldn't have minded having genes for being taller and good at sports and more self-confident. Alycia genes.

"What about plants?" Matt asked.

The question seemed to come out of nowhere. "What about them?" Plants were green and leafy; if they had three shiny leaves, they might be poison ivy. That pretty much covered the topic of plants for Maggie.

"If you won't kill animals because they're alive, why do you kill plants? They're just as alive as animals."

Uh-oh. Maggie should have known that Matt wouldn't be looking to discuss the best way to raise African violets. "Not *just* as alive."

"*Just* as alive. You're either alive, or you're not. Plants are as alive as you can get."

"But . . ." Why *didn't* Maggie refuse to kill plants? Well, for one thing, if she didn't eat plants, what *would* she eat? Even tofu was made out of some kind of plant—what kind, Maggie couldn't begin to imagine.

And it didn't seem wrong to eat plants. It didn't. But there had to be more to it than that. Maggie tried to think harder.

"Plants don't feel and animals do. I know, you said Squirmy didn't really feel things, he just reacted to things, but I think he *did* feel things, really feel them. Plants don't."

"So it's feeling that makes the big difference? Not just living, like you said before?"

Maggie nodded. This time she was pretty sure she was right.

"Why? What's so special about feeling?"

Why? Maggie remembered back to kindergarten when you could answer *Why?* with *Because. Why* did feeling matter? Maggie had never known that there were questions that were so hard.

"Well, if you don't feel anything—like, if you're a rock—then it really doesn't matter what happens to you. People can kick you up and down the street and it's okay, because you don't even know that anybody's kicking you. And I don't think plants can feel. They're more like rocks that way. But if you *do* feel things, then it does matter. What happens to you. Even if all you feel is really simple things, like a worm just lying there, feeling the squishiness of nice, warm mud. If you can feel, you have a right to keep on feeling."

Matt thought for a minute. Maggie wondered if his brain hurt as much as hers did.

"Do you eat eggs?" he asked then. There was something in his tone that made her wary.

"Uh-huh. You don't have to kill a chicken to get its eggs. And an egg—well, maybe it could turn into a chicken someday, but when it's still an egg, it doesn't feel anything."

"Milk? Cheese? Butter?" Matt was plainly enjoying himself now.

"I'm not a vegan," Maggie said, proud that she knew the word.

"Have you ever read anything about how they treat the chickens and cows that give you the eggs and milk you eat?"

"No," Maggie said slowly. She could tell she wasn't going to like the direction the conversation was taking.

"It's not pretty," Matt said. "You think your milk comes from Bossy the Cow? And your eggs from a happy mother hen scratching around in the barnyard with all her animal friends, maybe singing some Disney-style songs and doing little animated dances? Think again. Factory farms. That's where your eggs and milk come from. They keep the chickens all day and all night in little tiny cages with four chickens crammed into a cage. They have to cut their beaks off so they don't peck each other to death. The chickens never see the light of day. So much for *their* feelings."

Halfway through Matt's outburst, Maggie had put her hands over her ears, trying to shut out the sound of Matt's voice, but he kept on talking louder, as if it were all Maggie's fault that animals were treated that way, as if she were personally responsible for the fate of every caged chicken.

"And cows," Matt went on, obviously enjoying his role as grim realist breaking the bad news to a starry-eyed idealist. "Believe me, the cows that make the milk you're drinking now"—he tapped Maggie's milk carton with an accusing finger—"don't spend long lazy days grazing in the meadows, smelling the clover and munching on daisies. They're chained in their stalls, slaves to the milking machine. If feelings are so important, what about *their* feelings?"

"Why are you telling me this?" Maggie asked in an agitated voice. "I bet it isn't even true."

"It's true all right," Matt said. "I saw a whole program about it on PBS."

"Oh, if it was on TV, then it *has* to be true." But the sarcasm fell flat. It all probably *was* true. Matt had sounded so sure of himself.

"There're tons of books on this stuff, too."

"Well, what am I supposed to do about it?" What *could* she do about it?

"For starters, don't act like you're Miss Goody-Good because you don't dissect animals. You say that feelings are what matter. Well, Squirmy didn't feel *anything* when we killed him."

"When *you* killed him," Maggie corrected.

"But factory farm animals—the ones that produce the milk and eggs and butter and cheese you eat every day—are miserable every minute of their lives."

"Hold on." Matt's self-righteous anger was too much. "*You* eat eggs. *You* drink milk."

"Yes, and *I* don't go around telling other people they shouldn't be doing dissections."

Maggie felt close to tears. She felt as bruised and battered as a boxer leaving the ring after a losing round. Matt had definitely won today's argument, though Maggie held on fiercely to the thought that when all was said and done, he was no better than she was. However wrong it was to eat animal products, it had to be worse to eat animal products *and* to eat meat *and* to dissect animals. Because you couldn't save all animals, did that mean you shouldn't save any?

But, as of this minute, Maggie wasn't going to eat milk or eggs or cheese or butter anymore. Or honey?

She had become a vegan.

After school, Jake was waiting for Maggie again. Had he noticed that Alycia was absent today? The weather had turned sunny and quite warm for January, and Monday's snow was beginning to melt into muddy slush.

"Are you in a big hurry?" Jake asked. He gestured toward the bleachers next to the middle-school soccer field. "Can you hang out for a while?"

Maggie was too surprised by the request to refuse, even if she had wanted to refuse, which she didn't. She felt oddly wicked as she let Jake lead the way to the bleachers. Being alone with Jake was almost like smoking a cigarette—or at least like holding an unlit cigarette in her hand. It felt daring and disreputable. It felt like something Alycia would never do.

Maggie wondered what Jake wanted to talk about. But when they were seated together on the top row of the highest bleacher, he didn't say anything. Was Maggie supposed to say something?

"How's it going?" she finally said, once the silence had gone on long enough to make her feel even more self-conscious. Not a brilliant opener, but better than nothing.

"Okay," Jake said. "How 'bout you?" Another dazzling line.

"Okay." Maggie resisted the urge to push back the strand of dark hair that had fallen down over his eye.

"You were talking to Dixon at lunch. You like him or something?"

"He was just helping me with my opinion essay. It's on dissections, and he's for them and I'm against them, and, you know, Ms. Bealer says we have to put in the other side. So that's why I was talking to Matt."

Jake didn't say anything else. As the silence started to stretch on again, Maggie summoned all her conversational resources and asked, too cheerfully, "What are you writing your essay on?"

Jake gave a low, bitter laugh. "Like I'd bother to write one. Nobody in this school gives a damn about my opinions."

"I do." Did she? What else could she say? She couldn't very well say: Yup, well, that's true. And she *had* been wondering about Jake for days, what went on behind those eyes, why he would be the only person in the biology class to see what she saw and feel what she felt.

Jake reached over and took her hand. Maggie almost tumbled off the bleachers in shock. No boy had ever held her hand before. She felt acutely uncomfortable: she barely knew Jake; she hadn't spoken ten sentences to him in her whole entire life. And yet in a strange way she had as much in common with him as she did with Alycia—Alycia who still had a father and a perfect A average in biology class.

"You're different from the others," Jake said.

"I am?" Maggie tried to ease her hand away, but she

81

could tell that she would have to tug pretty hard to release it, and she didn't want to hurt Jake's feelings. Nor was the sensation of his warm fingers around hers totally unpleasant.

"You care about things, about people. You even care about *worms.*" Jake gave his dark laugh again. "I guess if you can care about worms, you can care about anything. Including my half-assed opinions. Maggie McIntosh, the all-purpose carer."

To Maggie's mingled relief and disappointment, he let go of her hand. She quickly put it in her jumper pocket, giving a little shiver so that Jake would think she had hidden her hand because the afternoon was growing chilly, not because she was afraid he might try to hold it again.

"You cold?"

"A little bit." She was wearing only a sweater, and the sun was sinking low in the cloud-streaked sky.

Jake slipped off his black leather jacket and draped it over her shoulders. "Better?"

Maggie nodded. She had never felt more tense and awkward in her life. And yet . . . there was something undeniably romantic about a boy offering her his jacket. She tried to think of Matt offering her his jacket—offering her anything—and failed completely.

"Are you going to do the fish dissection?" Jake asked.

"No. What about you?"

"Same here. Another F." Jake said it with perverse satisfaction. Maggie wondered which he wanted more: not to do the dissection or to lay claim to another failing grade.

"I don't believe in killing living things," Jake said, his voice low and earnest. The heat of his body was still in his jacket. Maggie felt its tingling warmth on her shoulders.

"Me neither," she said. "But . . ." She was going to ask him about killing plants, then thought better of it. She had dealt enough with Matt's questions for one day.

"But?"

"Then why do you smoke?" she asked instead. "If you don't want to kill things, why do you smoke?"

Jake shrugged. "It's a habit, I guess. A bad habit. Or maybe I don't want to kill *other* things."

"I have to go," Maggie said. She did have to go. Her mother was going to be home early, and they were going to the mall to shop for shoes. She handed Jake his jacket. "Thanks."

They climbed down the bleachers. Maggie stumbled once, in her nervousness not to look clumsy in front of Jake. He steadied her with his hand.

"Well, goodbye," Maggie said when they reached the bottom.

"Tell your pal Alycia that I'm not so bad," Jake said.

"I will," Maggie promised. She smiled at Jake. He *wasn't* so bad. He really wasn't.

Usually it took Maggie forever to find a pair of shoes that she and her mother both liked, but that day they were lucky and ended up buying the second pair Maggie tried on.

"This calls for ice cream," her mother said.

Ice cream. Made from milk. Milk from unhappy cows.

"I don't think I feel like ice cream today," Maggie said feebly.

"My daughter? Not feel like ice cream?"

"Not today. Really, I'm not very hungry."

"Maggie." Her mother's use of her real name signaled the seriousness of what she was about to say next. "Are you on a diet?" She turned Maggie so that she could look into her face. "You weigh—what? Ninety pounds? Tell me you're not on a diet. If you're on a diet, I'm going to— It's the *media*. How skinny do women today have to be? Ninety pounds isn't skinny enough? Maggles, those models you see in magazines, that's not how women, let alone *girls*, are supposed to look. I mean it, I'm going to—"

"I'm not on a diet."

Maggie wasn't sure her mother would even hear her, mid-tirade, but she did.

"You'd tell me if you were? So many young girls, they *say* they're not on a diet, but all they drink is diet soda, and they're off weighing themselves ten times a day—"

It was best to tell her and get it over with. "I'm a vegan."

This time her mother didn't hear, Maggie spoke so softly.

"A what?"

"A vegan. You know, like the people at the conference—the ones you hate . . ."

For a moment, her mother looked stunned. Maggie knew what she was thinking: *Dear God, what did I ever do to deserve a daughter who is a vegan?* Finally her mother said, "Why? May I at least ask why?"

"It's sort of a long story. Well, you know I don't eat meat anymore. And Matt says that it's really worse to eat eggs and milk products than to eat meat, because at least when they kill animals they do it quickly, while animals on factory farms are in terrible pain all the time."

"Matt said this."

"Matt Dixon. He's my lab partner in biology."

"What does he eat?"

"Oh, he eats everything."

"But he doesn't think you should eat anything?"

"He didn't say *that*. I told you, it's a long story. But, anyway, I don't think I'm like those conference people. Because I still eat honey. I don't think it hurts the bees when we take it—though I guess they're pretty disappointed when they get back to the hive and find it's all gone."

"Maggie, you tell Mr. Matt, for me, that there are such things as free-range chickens—happy chickens who are allowed to run free, laying happy eggs. From now on, that's what we'll buy. They sell them at Olson's dairy, right off Route Eleven. Yes, your old-fashioned family farm, where they also happen to keep happy cows. I believe they keep happy bees there, too. And, for your future reference, I do not hate the vegans attending Bob's conference. I merely find them extremely self-righteous and annoying. Which is how I suspect I'd find your friend Matt."

"So you're not mad?"

"I am not mad. But I *am* hungry. So let's stop at Olson's on the way home. I'm in the mood for a huge, fluffy, cheesy, eggy omelette."

Maggie gave her a grateful hug. "Me too."

9

Maggie worked on her opinion essay all through the long Martin Luther King, Jr., weekend. She usually wasn't the type to brag, but when she read over the final draft, freshly printed from the computer, she did think, in all honesty, that it was the most convincing essay ever written in the history of the world. Anyone reading it would definitely give up eating meat and unhappy-animal products forever, and never do a dissection again.

As she read the essay a second time on Monday afternoon, lovingly adding a few commas and semicolons here and there, the phone rang. Maggie picked it up.

"Hi, Maggie," a boy's voice said. It sounded like

Jake, probably too cool to bother saying his name. Maggie hated it when people didn't identify themselves on the phone. It was rude and arrogant to assume that everyone in the whole world would recognize your voice instantly.

But of course Maggie *had* recognized Jake's voice instantly. She remained silent, waiting for Jake to do his part.

"You don't know who this is, do you?"

Maggie still refused to answer.

"It's Jake."

"Hi, Jake." Maggie thawed a bit. The only boy who had ever held her hand was also the only boy who had ever called her on the phone. And he did have a great voice—low and confidential, as if whatever he was saying was meant for her alone.

"What're you doing?"

"Nothing much. Working on my opinion essay. I just finished it." She could close her eyes now and see how her essay would look printed in the typeface of *The Grand Valley Gazette.*

"You really go in for prizes and stuff, don't you?"

Was that an accusation? Some people *liked* to be good students. Some people thought it was a sacrifice, not an accomplishment, to be getting F's on every biology lab.

"What about you?" Maggie asked, to turn the conversation back to Jake. "What are you doing?"

"Hanging out. Thinking about you." Maggie caught in her breath. "That was all I called to say. That I was thinking about you."

Maggie didn't say anything. What was she supposed to say? *Thanks.* Or: *What were you thinking?* Or: *I was thinking about you, too.* Silence on the phone was even more uncomfortable than silence in person. On the phone you couldn't see the person—his gestures, the look on his face, whether or not he was smiling. It was odd to be holding on so tightly to the receiver, listening to . . . nothing.

"Well, I gotta go," Jake said finally. "See you tomorrow, I guess."

"Tomorrow," Maggie echoed softly. Jake hung up first, then, after a long moment, Maggie.

"Who was that?" her mother called to her from the kitchen.

"A boy from school." Maggie tried to say it casually, as if boys called her all the time.

"A *boy* from school?" Her mother stood in the doorway now, obviously interested. "I hope it wasn't Matt What's-His-Name, with more menu advice."

"No, it was a different boy."

"What did he want?"

"Nothing," Maggie said. But she knew that the smile that insisted on hovering around her mouth was giving her away.

In biology class on Tuesday, Maggie began to feel the fish dissection drawing near. Mr. O. kept making little references to it. "When you dissect your perch on Friday, you'll see . . ." "One thing I want you to look for on Friday is . . ." At each mention of Friday, Maggie flinched. Did she have to tell Mr. O. that she wouldn't be doing this dissection, either? Or would he figure it out when he saw her sitting stiffly in class Friday morning, staring straight ahead as Matt cut into the gleaming belly of the cold, dead fish? When he did figure it out, would he be more or less angry than he'd been when she refused to dissect Squirmy?

At least the fish Matt would be dissecting didn't have a name. He wouldn't be dissecting Perchy.

The opinion essay was due on Wednesday, so Tuesday's English class was spent in what Ms. Bealer called "peer critique groups." In peer critique groups, students shared their work with one another in small groups and commented on it. It was always scary for Maggie reading her work aloud to other kids in the class, but sometimes they had helpful things to say. Ms. Bealer had a rule that all the criticism offered had to be *constructive* criticism.

Both Matt and Alycia were in Maggie's English class, and that day they were both in her peer critique group, as well. Jake had English a different period; the only classes he had with Maggie were biology and art, and she had barely noticed him in either of those until the last couple of weeks, when she had started to notice him everywhere.

Alycia read her essay first. It was beautifully written, like all Alycia's essays, and it was full of vivid and memorable facts about waste in America. Maggie had never realized before how much unnecessary packaging there was in the world. She was going to tell her mother that, in addition to buying free-range eggs and family-farm milk, they were going to have to carry their own reusable canvas sacks to the grocery store and buy bulk macaroni and flour and spices.

After Alycia finished reading, Maggie couldn't think of any constructive criticism to offer. When her turn in the circle came, first she gave an honest compliment: "It's wonderful." Ms. Bealer said they were always supposed to begin with a compliment.

"But . . ." Maggie wasn't sure how to put her finger on what was missing in Alycia's essay. It was just too *easy* to argue against needless waste. Was there anyone left on the planet who thought waste was *good*? "I was just wondering. Is there, like, anything to be said on the *other* side?"

"I couldn't think of anything," Alycia said. Which wasn't surprising, as there was nothing to think of.

"Well, then, it's a great essay," Maggie concluded.

Matt didn't have much to say about Alycia's essay, either. All he told her was that one of the facts in her second paragraph really belonged in her third paragraph, and Alycia agreed that it did.

Matt's essay on genetic research was wonderful, too. The unwelcome thought struck Maggie that there was going to be a lot of competition for the opinion essay prizes. In her peer critique group alone, there were two essays as good—almost as good?—as hers. And that was in one critique group in one class taught by one teacher.

But Matt's essay left Maggie somehow unconvinced. Matt thought it was fine to go ahead and change people genetically, adding a gene here and subtracting a gene there to make people taller, healthier, smarter. Everything Matt said sounded true enough, and every sentence rang with his characteristic scorn for anyone who thought differently. Still, when Matt finished reading, Maggie didn't feel like running out and having herself genetically altered.

"It's very well written," Maggie said, for Matt's compliment. "But it made me wonder: Don't you think changing people that way is—doesn't it seem like playing God?"

"People intervene in the course of nature all the time," Matt said impatiently. "You get a strep throat, you take antibiotics. Is that playing God? People used to die of polio, and smallpox, and TB. Now they don't. Were the scientists who invented the vaccines playing God?"

"But don't you think changing people's *genes* is different?"

"No," Matt said.

The bluntness of his answer irked Maggie. *Fine*, she wanted to say. *Don't listen to any criticism. Assume that anyone who offers you constructive criticism is a raving idiot.*

The other three people in the group read essays on seat-belt laws, smoking, and censorship. None of their essays were anywhere near as good as Alycia's or Matt's. Maggie's turn came last. Her voice shook as she read the first paragraph of her essay, but it grew stronger as she continued to read. As she heard her own arguments unfolding, one after another, she convinced herself all over again of the essential *rightness* of what she was saying. When she was finished, she looked at Matt. Was *he* convinced now? How could he not be? But all along, Matt had acted as if everything Maggie said and thought and did was worthless.

"It's great, Maggie." The honest admiration in Matt's voice caught Maggie by surprise. "You *almost* had me convinced."

"Almost?"

"Well, I have to say I find the arguments you give for the other side strangely appealing. But it's a great essay. I wouldn't change a thing. Except maybe the conclusion."

Maggie knew that Matt was teasing about the conclusion, but she could tell he sincerely meant the praise. And, she was discovering, compliments from Matt Dixon were as pleasurable as they were rare.

The others in the group agreed with Matt's appraisal. Alycia said, "I'm so glad I didn't do the worm dissection! I'm not going to do the fish dissection, either. You're going to win the contest, Maggie. You're going to get first prize for the whole seventh grade."

"We could *all* win," Maggie said, shy in the face of so much praise. "They're giving out six prizes total, including the three honorable mentions. And there are six of us in our group. We could all win."

Ms. Bealer stopped by their cluster of chairs. "How are you progressing? Have our constructive critics been doing their job?"

Maggie smiled at her. "We think we're *all* going to win the essay contest."

"Do you know who the judges are going to be?" Alycia asked.

"The other English teachers and I thought the contest would be more fair if we weren't judging our own students' essays. So we've asked three other teachers to serve as judges this year: Ms. Bellon, Ms. Kocik, and

Mr. O'Neill. The winners will be announced at the end of next week."

It took a full second for the name to register.

Mr. O'Neill.

Mr. O.

Finally, on Thursday, as the end-of-class bell was ringing, Mr. O. called out over the commotion, "Maggie, I'd like to talk to you for a minute."

Here it comes, Maggie thought.

Once the others had left, Mr. O. motioned to Maggie to sit down. "I'll write you a late pass for lunch," he said. So this time he wasn't inviting her to have lunch with him. Well, he couldn't have lunch with students every day. How many other Grand Valley students had eaten lunch with a teacher even once?

Maggie sat down in her regular first-row seat. Mr. O. pulled his chair around in front of his desk, so it was next to her lab table, and straddled it backward. The casual posture suggested a low-key, friendly conversation, but there was something in Mr. O.'s eyes that didn't look low-key and friendly.

Yet his tone, when he began talking, was as gentle and caring as ever. "So. Maggie. Tomorrow. The fish dissection. Will you let Matt and me help you do it?"

Miserably, Maggie shook her head. Part of her

wanted to say yes, to say whatever Mr. O. wanted her to say, to thank him for caring about her enough to use his lunch period to try to talk to her one more time. But a bigger part of her needed to say no.

"What am I going to do with you?" It sounded like something her mother would say; it sounded like something a father would say. "You're too good a student to fail this course. Believe me, Maggie, there's no one I want *less* to fail than you. But if you keep on getting F's in the labs, you'll leave me no other choice. Does your mother know that you're in danger of failing?"

Maggie nodded. "I mean, I told her I'm not doing the dissections. But—is there anything else I could do instead? Like a report for extra credit?"

"This is a *lab* course. In a lab course, we do *labs*."

"Why do all the labs have to involve killing something?" Maggie tried to sound as scornful as Matt would sound, but she knew she sounded close to tears instead.

"No one in our class will be killing a fish. The perch will be prepared for dissection before they're delivered here."

"That makes it better? That someone else kills them?"

"I thought your objection was to killing." Mr. O.'s voice had that angry edge to it now.

96

"Yes, but killing is killing, whoever does it. It's no less killing because someone else does it for you."

"This girlish sentimentality is going to cost you your education in biology." The coldness in Mr. O.'s voice was as sharp as the scalpels that would cut open dozens of innocent, once-living fish tomorrow.

"Jake's not dissecting things, either, and he's not a girl."

"Jacob Dycus is a very troubled young man. I would hardly recommend him as a role model."

"At least he doesn't kill things."

"Maggie, listen to me. I've been teaching biology for twenty years now. For twenty years I've been dissecting animals and supervising student dissections. Think about it. If dissecting animals is such a terrible crime, what does that make me?"

Maggie said nothing. The unanswered question hung in the air between them.

Mr. O. stood up and returned to his desk. He scribbled out a late pass for lunch and another pass for Friday, for the library. "Don't bother coming to class tomorrow. We'll see you Monday."

Through her film of tears, Maggie fled to the hall. Mr. O. was a mass murderer, a cold-blooded killer of hundreds of worms, fish, and frogs. Why should she care what he thought of her?

But she did. The memory of the special smile he had

once had for her, not so very long ago, choked her. Her only hope was that when he read her essay he'd understand. Maybe he wouldn't agree—even after reading it, Matt still didn't agree with her—but at least he'd understand. If only he would understand enough not to hate her for doing what she had to do. If only he would understand enough so that everything between the two of them could be the way it used to be.

10

When Maggie reached the library on Friday morning, for her exile from biology, Jake wasn't there. Maybe he had gone to class; maybe Mr. O. hadn't had time to talk to him yesterday about the fish dissection the way he had talked to Maggie. It was odd, in a way, that he hadn't asked Jake to stay after class, too. But perhaps he wanted to talk to each of the rebels alone.

Jake came in as Maggie was opening her biology book. She planned to use the library time to study for the upcoming exam, hoping that if she got an A on every single exam, Mr. O. wouldn't have the heart to give her an F on her report card.

"Where were you?" Jake asked as he sat down next to her at her table by the window. Maggie noticed that

Jake had no books with him. It was probably uncool to carry books.

"Mr. O. told me yesterday to come here."

"He didn't tell me. I guess he wanted the pleasure of kicking me out of class in front of everybody. Public humiliation is one of his things."

"Did he ask you if you were going to do the dissection, and you refused?"

"You might put it that way. I called him a fascist."

"Oh, Jake." Maggie was glad she had been spared that encounter. Maybe Mr. O. still did like her, at least a little bit, since he had let her go quietly to the library instead of expelling her publicly. "What did he say?"

"He threw me out for a week. Boohoo, boohoo. A whole week without his corny jokes and his crazy ties. My heart is breaking in two. And all his big threats. He's going to give me an F. I'm already getting an F. That's what gets him. There's nothing he can do to me." Jake laughed mirthlessly. "Nothing I haven't already done to myself."

But there was plenty Mr. O. could do to Maggie. He could take the A she was so proud of and turn it into an F. Maggie still didn't believe he would really do it. It would be too unfair. He could give her an F for every lab she missed, but labs were supposed to be only 20 percent of their grade. If 80 percent of her grade was an A, and 20 percent was an F, her final grade should be—

100

Maggie did some quick math in her head—a B. It would be too unfair to give her an F when she had earned a B. Mr. O. might have some faults—three weeks ago Maggie would have denied it, but she couldn't deny it now—but he wasn't *unfair*.

"Let's get out of here," Jake said.

Maggie didn't understand. "Now?" They couldn't leave school now; it was only fourth period. They were supposed to be in the library.

"No, next year. *Yes,* now. I feel like having a cigarette. Besides, it's almost sixty degrees today. We don't need to sit here in this pathetic library. We could be out watching the snowdrifts melt away."

"We can't go outside. We don't have a pass."

"You don't get it, do you? We don't need a pass. This isn't a maximum-security prison, even though they act like it is. Who's going to stop us? Do you see any armed guards? Any attack dogs? Any electric fences? That old library guy isn't even watching us. Nobody is. Come on, Maggie. This is our chance. They're cutting up dead fish in here. Let's go commune with life out there."

"But—"

"No buts."

Maggie gave in. Her heart was pounding as she silently packed up her books and followed Jake into the hall. Grand Valley Middle School didn't have any armed guards or attack dogs, but it did have hall monitors. What would Jake say if somebody stopped them? But nobody did. The only monitor they passed was deep in conversation with a teacher. It was incredibly easy to walk right out of the building and into the warm, welcoming January sun.

As soon as they were outside, Jake grabbed Maggie's hand. This time, now that she was psychologically prepared for it, it felt very nice to have his fingers intertwined with hers. It felt like the two of them against the world, the forces of life against the forces of death.

With his free hand, Jake pulled out a pack of cigarettes.

"Don't smoke," Maggie said.

"Why not? Once we cross the street, we won't be on school property."

"You said you wanted to commune with life. Smoking kills people."

Jake stuffed the cigarettes back in his pocket. "You speak, and I obey."

They had reached the little park across the street from the middle school. "Climb that tree," Maggie commanded, to test her new powers.

Jake dropped her hand and swung himself easily to a perch on the lowest branch. Maggie laughed.

"Come on up." The branch was sturdy enough to hold them both.

"I'm not very good at climbing." Unlike graceful Alycia, Maggie was a total klutz. She still remembered her terror of the jungle gym on the elementary-school playground. She should ask Matt if there was a gene for jungle-gym-phobia.

"I'll help you. Here." Jake leaped lightly from the tree and offered Maggie his two cupped hands as a stirrup. In an instant, he had boosted her up; in another instant, he was seated beside her, their shoulders touching, her hand back in his.

"This," Jake said, "is much nicer than the library."

Maggie couldn't disagree. For the first time since Maggie had known him, Jake looked happy—not sullen or surly or bored, just happy. Then, as she turned toward him to reply, he kissed her. It wasn't a long kiss, but it was definitely a kiss. Maggie's first kiss—just a week and a half before her thirteenth birthday.

From across the street, they heard the bell ring. Fourth period was over.

"I have to go," Maggie said regretfully.

"Why?"

"I just do."

Maggie was afraid Jake would argue, but he didn't. He let himself down first and held out his arms to her. Maggie jumped into them, like an old-fashioned lady alighting from a stagecoach.

"See you later, Maggie." To her relief, he didn't sound mad; he still looked foolishly happy.

"You're not coming?"

"Nah. I've had enough for one day. Study hard. Be good," he said in a voice that seemed both mocking and tender.

As Maggie slipped back into the school, she wondered: What would Alycia say if she knew that Maggie had cut class and been kissed on the lips—by Jake Dycus?

"I got another F today in biology," Maggie told her mother that night at dinner. They were each slurping a big bowl full of cold cereal and sliced bananas and happy-cow milk. When they were both too tired to face fixing any real food, they would eat cereal for dinner. Sometimes Maggie's mother called the cereal suppers "not my finest moment of motherhood." But usually she defended them: "If those food pyramid people want us to eat *six* servings a day of grains and cereals, they're going to have to expect an occasional cereal entrée."

"Oh, Maggie," her mother said now, laying down her spoon. "That makes how many? Two F's? What's going to happen to your grade?"

"Mr. O. says if I don't do any of the dissections, he'll give me an F."

"For the whole trimester?"

"That's what he says."

"That's ridiculous. Did you ask him if you could make up the labs in some other way?"

"Uh-huh. He said no. I think he's really, really into dissections."

"What about your classmates? Are the rest of them busily hacking up dead worms and—what else?"

"Fish. Everyone except me, and Alycia, and this one boy, Jake."

"The boy who called you on the phone." Maggie's mother took one glance at Maggie's face and chortled with satisfaction. "Am I good or am I good?"

"It was Jake," Maggie admitted reluctantly. She had a grudging respect for her mother's flashes of intuition, but she didn't like giving her mother so much uninvited access to her life.

"What kind of boy is he?"

"He's . . ." Maggie tried to think of a truthful answer that wouldn't sound defensive. She gave up. "He's just a boy."

"Good student?"

"Not exactly. I bet he could be, but he has this chip on his shoulder, and he won't let anybody make him do anything he doesn't want to do." Maggie knew that she had already said too much.

"I get the picture. You like him, don't you?"

"Sort of."

"When do I get to meet him?"

Never. "I barely know him." Though Maggie had to admit that she knew Jake well enough to let him kiss her.

"What does Alycia think of him?"

Maggie hesitated. "He's not her type."

"But he's *your* type? Your type is underachievers with chips on their shoulders?" Her mother gave an exaggerated sigh as she shoved her cereal bowl away. "Remember, Maggie: Mistake Number One, throwing yourself away on a loser."

Maggie bristled at the word. Who was her mother to disparage Maggie's friends? Who was her mother to disparage Maggie's *father*? She seemed to forget that the man she was putting down happened to be the only father Maggie had ever had, even if his place in her life had been reduced to the size of a shoe box.

"Jake's dad left, too." Maggie wasn't sure why she said it. Maybe it was because her mother always seemed to think she was the only one who had gotten dumped when Maggie's father disappeared. That all the loss and hurt had been hers alone.

"A match made in heaven!" her mother said. "Both of you from broken homes, both of you sabotaging your biology grades for some quixotic crusade."

Maggie gave her mother a blank look. She didn't

know what the word meant, but she could tell it wasn't a compliment.

"Quixotic. From *Don Quixote*. It's a famous book about a crackpot who thinks he's a knight in shining armor and goes around fighting windmills."

"That's what you think I'm doing?"

"I didn't say that. Well, maybe I did say that. Do you really think your failing biology is going to change the world?"

"If bad things are happening in the world, we have to at least *try* to stop them. I mean, we can't just do *nothing.*"

Maggie's mother reached out her hand to Maggie. "Oh, Mags, forget everything I just said. I'm glad you're still idealistic. Stay that way as long as you can."

Even though her mother didn't sound sarcastic anymore, she still sounded condescending, as if caring about killing animals was a cute phase a starry-eyed young person would go through on her way to becoming a tough, cynical, hard-boiled adult.

"One thing I'd like to know, though," her mother said as she carried both bowls to the dishwasher. "You said Alycia isn't doing the dissections, either? Don't tell me Bob Eagen's daughter is going to get an F in biology, too."

"Her lab partner does them for her."

Maggie's mother burst out laughing. "It's perfect! Like father, like daughter. Get someone else to do your scut work for you—your lab partner, your secretary. I love it! But not my daughter, oh, no, she's the one out there fighting the windmills. I guess I'm proud of you for it." She gave Maggie a hug. "Don't let Jake call the shots, though."

Maggie pulled away. "What's wrong with Jake? You don't even know him. I've barely said two sentences to you about him."

"Maybe I don't know Jake. What I do know is that some people fight windmills to try to change the world. Some people fight them because they like to fight, and if someone gets hurt in the process, all the better. And some of us stopped fighting years ago because we've learned the hard way that the windmill always wins."

The weather turned cold and snowy again. Jake called Maggie twice over the weekend. He wanted her to go out for a walk with him in the snow, but Maggie told him that her mother said no. It was only half a lie: Maggie hadn't asked her mother if she could go out with Jake, but she suspected that if she *had* asked, the answer would have been no. At the least, her mother would have insisted on meeting Jake first, and then Maggie had the uncomfortable feeling that, with his jacket and his hair and his sullen expression, Jake would look exactly the way her mother expected him to. And Maggie couldn't stand giving her mother that much satisfaction.

Besides, Maggie was secretly relieved to have an excuse for why she couldn't see Jake alone. Maggie was increasingly drawn to Jake, but there was something stressful, something unsettling, about being with him.

Instead Maggie spent her Sunday afternoon baking cookies and knitting companionably with Alycia at Alycia's house, while outside the snow fell steadily, covering the bleachers where Jake had first held Maggie's hand, blanketing the tree branch where he had kissed her.

Alycia's father drove Maggie home toward nightfall. For all that Maggie's mother complained about Professor Eagen, Maggie liked him. Of course he would expect his secretary to type and file and take care of pesky little conference details: that was why people had secretaries, to do the work they didn't want to do. If Professor Eagen did all those things himself, her mother would be out of a job. Naturally, Maggie never said this to her mother. But she privately didn't think that Professor Eagen sounded so bad.

"Alycia tells me you're leading a revolt against animal dissections," he said as he backed out of their two-car garage. The Eagens never had to worry about shoveling their cars out of snowdrifts. One touch of their remote-controlled garage-door opener, and off they went.

"Well, sort of." Maggie hardly saw herself as the leader of a revolt, but she was flattered that Alycia had described her that way.

"Good for you," he said heartily, his approval a welcome contrast to her mother's ambivalence. "Did you know that a number of schools have eliminated animal dissections on ethical grounds? They use computer simulations or video instruction. Instead of a hundred students stumbling and bumbling through a botched dissection of a hundred animals, the same hundred students watch a video of an expertly done, professional dissection of a single animal. A lot of animal lives are saved that way. Sometimes I think that a century from now, people will look back on our treatment of nonhuman animals the same way we look back on the practice of slavery."

"Do you really?" If only Professor Eagen would tell this to Mr. O. Maybe Mr. O. would take Maggie's arguments more seriously if a grownup man—a Ph.D. college professor—shared them. She wondered if Mr. O. had read her essay yet. The contest winners were supposed to be announced sometime next week.

"I do. Of course, that's the historian in me, always

wondering what future historians are going to be saying about *us*."

Maggie thanked him warmly when he dropped her off at home, as much for his encouragement as for the ride. If this was what fathers were like, she definitely wouldn't mind having one.

On Monday, Mr. O. didn't smile at Maggie, and she didn't guess the answer to the light bulb joke: "How many paranoids does it take to change a light bulb?" "Who wants to know?" The class was moving on to frogs, with a frog dissection scheduled for a week from Friday. Maggie couldn't even imagine dissecting something that *hopped*. Hadn't Mr. O. ever read the *Frog and Toad* books? Hadn't he read *The Tale of Mr. Jeremy Fisher*?

The week wore on, with no smiles from Mr. O. Twice after school, when Alycia had basketball practice, Maggie sat with Jake in the bleachers again. Together they brushed off the snow from the topmost bleacher—*their* bleacher—clearing just a few feet of bare metal, so that they had to sit very close together. They still didn't talk much; Maggie had yet to tell Jake about her father. Jake held her hand the whole time, tucking it safe and warm into his jacket pocket. But he didn't kiss her.

Friday morning, Maggie listened tensely to morning announcements. If the contest winners were going to be announced this week, they would have to be announced today, though perhaps Ms. Bealer was going to announce them later on, in English class.

Finally, following a long list of notices about basketball, wrestling, the science fair, and the math team, Maggie heard Mr. Dworkin say, "I am pleased to announce the winners of the first annual seventh-grade opinion essay contest." Maggie clenched her hands so tightly that her nails dug into her palms. This was it.

"First prize, Kate Tyler. Second prize, Alycia Eagen."

So Alycia's essay had come out ahead of hers, even though Alycia hadn't given any arguments for the other side.

"Third prize, Seth Tomacki. Honorable mention, Matt Dixon . . ."

Yay, Matt! But please, oh please, oh please, oh please, let my name be next.

". . . Rudy Fejer, and Sally Scott. Congratulations to six outstanding writers."

He hadn't read Maggie's name. Alycia and Matt had won, but Maggie hadn't, nothing, not even honorable mention.

Nothing. And one of the judges had been Mr. O.

11

Maggie saw Alycia in the hall on the way to first-period art. "Congratulations," she made herself say as enthusiastically as she could. At least this wasn't like the Academy Awards, where they had a close-up camera focused on all the losers' faces for the moment when the announcement was made. At least Maggie had had time to put on her fixed, forced, best-friend-of-the-winner smile.

Alycia accepted Maggie's hug. There was an awkward pause. Then Alycia said, "I can't believe you didn't win, too. I mean, I just don't get it."

"Well, maybe next time." Maggie kept her smile in place. She didn't want to spoil Alycia's triumph. And maybe Alycia's essay *had* been better than hers.

But it hadn't.

As Maggie took her seat at the art table, she felt someone's arms go around her from behind. Jake.

The two of them, as if by mutual agreement, had never touched each other in public, or given any sign that they were friends. The secrecy somehow added an extra dimension to their relationship, placing it beyond anybody else's scrutiny or judgment. Maggie still hadn't told another living soul that Jake had kissed her. So now it was a shock to feel his public embrace.

It lasted only a moment, and then he withdrew, before anybody else had a chance to see.

"Bummer," he said softly. Maggie knew he was talking about the contest. "I told you, they're all cretins, every last one of them. But we'll get even someday, wait and see."

Jake's obvious contempt for the judges should have made Maggie feel better, but in an odd way it made her feel worse. Not only had she lost the essay contest to Alycia but she had lost some different, unspoken contest to Jake. The judges' verdict seemed to show that she was wrong and foolish to have dreamed about the contest. She should have been like Jake, refusing to let herself care about winning in the first place. And Jake's remark about getting even sounded vaguely threatening. Maggie didn't want to get even with the world. She just wanted the world to appreciate her, at least as much as it appreciated Alycia.

In biology, Matt arrived at their lab table a few moments after Maggie.

"Congratulations!" Maggie said brightly. This time it came out easier.

"On what?" Matt asked. He didn't sound puzzled as much as angry.

"On the *essay* contest. Didn't you listen to morning announcements? You won honorable mention."

"I heard it."

"So congratulations!"

"You don't think it's strange that you didn't win?"

Of course Maggie thought it was strange that she hadn't won. She thought it was absolutely unbelievable that she hadn't won. But she also recognized that she might be the tiniest bit biased.

"I'm sure there were a lot of good essays," Maggie said, as if she were reciting a line from *The Good Loser's Handbook.* "Everybody couldn't win."

"Maggie, I *heard* yours. You might even say I helped you to *write* yours. And I'm telling you, it should have won. It was better than mine. It was ten times better than Alycia's. I don't know about the other kids who won; I haven't read their stuff. But your essay was better than at least two of the essays that did win. I know that for a fact."

Matt's indignation on her behalf helped more than Jake's had. Matt wouldn't have said she should have won if he hadn't believed it. Maggie knew from experience that Matt never said anything to make somebody feel better. If anything, Matt specialized in making people feel worse.

Mr. O. blew his whistle. Was Maggie right to think that he was avoiding her with his eyes? That he was looking everywhere except at the front-center lab table? "Campers! How many college football players does it take to change a light bulb?"

Maggie hardly listened to the answer: "The whole team, and they each get three credits for it." A terrible suspicion was stirring in her. Had Mr. O. voted against her essay for the prize because it disagreed with his own views? Had he downgraded her because he was angry at her for opposing dissections in his class and she had angered him further by daring to oppose them in her essay?

No. She remembered her own thoughts in his defense the other day: Mr. O. had his faults, but he wasn't unfair. He wouldn't have voted against her as a punishment for her protest. Alycia's essay *had* been beautifully written; Matt's, too. There was a large subjective element in judging any writing contest. You couldn't go around boo-hooing that the world was unfair every time someone honestly preferred someone else's essay to yours. Even with major prizes, like the Nobel Prize

116

in Literature, people disagreed all the time about who deserved to win.

"All right, campers," Mr. O. said. "Today I introduce to you—our classroom frog! The frogs we'll be dissecting will arrive prepared for dissection next Friday, but I'll be using this fellow here—he's a young male—for a special procedure called *pithing*, which has to be done on a live frog."

Maggie's heart, already overfull, swelled even further as Mr. O. carried a small terrarium from the windowsill to his desk. Unlike worms and fish, frogs were *cute*. The one on Mr. O.'s desk was an itty-bitty thing, no bigger than Maggie's fist. She could already sense his impatient, curious personality. He hopped against the glass eagerly, restlessly, as if to say, "There's a whole world out there I need to explore!" His goggly eyes were alert, inquiring. Maggie hadn't meant to name him, but, unbidden, a name came to her: Froggles.

Maggie hoped that whatever pithing was, it wasn't too terrible. But it certainly *sounded* terrible.

"What's pithing?" someone asked, so Maggie didn't have to.

"When you pith a frog, you cut off its head with a pair of scissors to get access to the spinal cord. That way you can pull on different nerves to see how the various muscles operate."

Maggie thought she was going to be sick.

"When it's alive?" Kip asked eagerly. "You cut off its head when it's alive?"

"That's right," Mr. O. said. "It all happens so quickly the frog feels no pain." Was this said for Maggie's benefit? "But it stays alive briefly afterward. That's what lets us observe the action of the nerves. I'll explain more about it between now and next Friday."

No. Mr. O. couldn't be serious. He was not going to cut off the head of a live frog in front of the class. But Mr. O. didn't seem to be joking. He acted as if pithing was common practice in biology. And, after all, every single frog that was killed for dissection was alive while it was being killed. Pithing was just another form of killing for the so-called sake of science.

Somehow Maggie endured the rest of class, trying not to think about Froggles's fate. But the only other thing she could fasten her thoughts on was the essay contest she had lost.

As soon as the bell rang, Matt turned to her. "Let's go."

Go where? But Maggie followed him out of the biology room, hoping Jake wasn't watching the two of them leave together.

"I want to get to the bottom of this," Matt said as he strode purposefully down the hall toward the front office and the teachers' room.

"The bottom of what?" Maggie had to hurry to keep up with him.

"Of the contest. You should have won, and you didn't win. I want to find out why."

Matt stopped in front of the teachers' room and rapped twice on the door. One of the P.E. teachers opened it.

"Is Ms. Bealer here?" Matt asked, as if he summoned teachers out of the teachers' room every day.

Ms. Bealer appeared in the doorway. "Matt, Maggie, what can I do for you?"

Maggie suddenly felt terribly embarrassed. What if everyone who'd lost the contest came whining about how he or she should have won? She could already hear Ms. Bealer's explanation for the judges' decision: *Well, Maggie, I'm afraid the judges simply didn't think that your essay was good enough. I'm sorry, dear.*

"We have a couple of questions about the judging of the essay contest," Matt replied.

Now Ms. Bealer, too, looked embarrassed. "I really don't have much information about it. As you know, I was not one of the judges myself. Ms. Bellon, Ms. Kocik, and Mr. O'Neill were our judges this year, and all three told me that it was very difficult to select only six winners. The judges' decision doesn't affect the grade you received on the essay as an assignment. I'm handing the essays back this afternoon: both of you received A+'s. Does this answer your questions?"

"No," Matt said.

"I'm sorry, dear. I wish I could be more helpful."

When Ms. Bealer had disappeared back into the teachers' room, Matt said, "We need to talk to the judges, to Bellon and Kocik."

Not to Mr. O. It was becoming obvious that Matt shared Maggie's suspicion, that it was Mr. O.'s disagreement with the conclusions of Maggie's essay that had cost her the prize.

"I don't want to," Maggie said. "I can't very well stand there and ask the judges point-blank: Why didn't I win?"

"I'll go talk to them by myself, then," Matt said. "I'll ask them point-blank: Why didn't she win?"

All through lunch, different kids stopped at their table to congratulate Alycia on her prize in the essay contest. Over and over again, Maggie listened to Alycia saying, "It was really a surprise to *me* that I won," and "I can't believe they picked *my* essay." Alycia was very good at sounding modest and humble. The strange thing was that Alycia really *was* modest and humble. Maggie couldn't remember ever hearing Alycia brag. Alycia didn't need to brag. She just smiled graciously as she accepted all the good things that the world laid at her feet.

In a break between congratulations, Alycia turned to Maggie. "I don't think I can dissect a *frog.*"

"Well, you didn't dissect a worm or a fish, either," Maggie told her. *You just made Kip do your dirty work for you, while you kept your A.*

"I know, but I sort of did. Mr. O. thinks I did. But a frog . . . That one Mr. O. is going to—do those things to—is awfully cute, Maggie."

"Don't dissect them at all, then. Tell Mr. O. You can come to the library with Jake and me." *If you're willing to pay the price.*

Maggie waited to see what Alycia would say. If Alycia had any conscience at all, any courage to back up her convictions, she would agree to join Maggie in her protest. There was a word for a person who believed one thing and did another. The word was *hypocrite.*

Alycia didn't reply right away. But the way she avoided meeting Maggie's eyes told what her answer would be.

"But it's like the frogs are already dead whether I dissect them or not," Alycia finally said. "If I refuse to do the dissection, I get an F and my frog is dead, anyway. No offense, Maggie, but I don't really see how that helps anything."

Maggie felt herself flushing. "I think it helps. If enough people say something is wrong, and say it loud enough, it has to help."

At least, Maggie hoped it would. But in a way, Alycia was right. So far Maggie had two F's in Mr. O.'s grade book, and Mr. O. had stopped liking her forever, and she had lost the essay contest, and her worm and her fish were still dead. What *had* she accomplished with her grand, noble protest against dissections? Had it been worth it?

Jake called Maggie that evening.

"You and Dixon were sure in a big hurry to run off together after biology."

Maggie had known Jake wouldn't like her leaving with Matt. But Jake's jealousy, predictable as it was, annoyed her. You didn't own somebody because you had kissed her once. Since that one kiss in the park, Jake hadn't kissed her again. Did he know that Maggie wasn't ready for anything too serious?

Although Maggie didn't feel like telling Jake the truth, she couldn't think how else to explain why she and Matt had gone racing off together.

"Matt thinks I should have won the essay contest, and he wanted to ask Ms. Bealer why I didn't win."

"How come he's so fired up about it?"

"I don't know. He just is."

"He likes you."

"Not that way."

"Yes, that way. What did Bealer say?"

"Nothing. She wasn't one of the judges. She doesn't know why I didn't win. It doesn't matter. Lots of people didn't win. I'm not the only one." Maybe Maggie should actually publish a handbook for good losers. She certainly was getting a lot of practice in the part.

"Do you like him?"

"Not that way," Maggie repeated.

"Not what way?"

Maggie didn't answer.

"You're supposed to say, 'Not the way I like you.' "

"Not the way I like you," Maggie repeated, hoping Jake could hear the smile in her voice over the phone. She didn't know if she liked Jake the way he wanted her to like him, but she *did* like him, and in a different way from the way in which she *did* like Matt.

"I've been thinking," Maggie said then. "About the frog dissection? Whether we dissect them or not, the frogs are all going to be killed, anyway. They're dead before they even get here. Except for Froggles, you know, the classroom frog. And Mr. O.'s going to—pith—him, whatever we do."

"What's your point? You're going to sell out and do the dissection this time?"

"No!" Maggie would never be like Alycia, never in a

million billion years. "I was just wondering—well, I wish there were something we *could* do. To make a real difference. Like really change how they teach biology in this school."

"Talk to Mr. O.," Jake said, and laughed a harsh laugh without any humor in it.

"Or at least—do you think we could save Froggles? Like—I don't know—frognap him or something so he won't get pithed? We can't let Mr. O. cut his head off. We can't."

"Let's save him," Jake said. "We can do it."

Maggie suddenly felt overwhelmed by what she had suggested. "How? Just take him out of the terrarium one day when Mr. O.'s not looking?"

"No, that guy sees everything. And we can't do it too soon, or he'll just get himself another frog to hack up. Here's what we'll do." Maggie heard an unaccustomed excitement in Jake's voice. "The day before the dissections, after the last bell rings, we'll hide out somewhere in the school, until all the teachers are gone and the custodians are taking their dinner break. Then we'll sneak back into the biology room, grab up Mr. Froggie, stick him in a sack, and hightail it out of there. Then when it's pithing time, there'll be no frog to pith. That should freak Mr. O. but good."

It really didn't sound much harder than walking out of the library had been on that last springlike morning.

But Maggie didn't want to "freak" Mr. O. She just wanted to save one innocent little frog from slaughter.

"I want to do it," Maggie said. Was this how John Hancock had felt when he signed the Declaration of Independence? As if he had changed the world forever by being willing, for one moment of one hour on one fateful day, to take a stand? Or as if he had just made the worst mistake in his life, but it was too late now to undo what he had done?

12

No sooner had Maggie hung up the phone from talking to Jake than it rang again. Maggie let her mother answer it.

"It's for you. Matt Dixon." Her mom put her hand over the receiver so Matt couldn't hear her next comment. "He called to tell you that King Soopers has a sale on tofu this week."

Maggie snatched the phone from her mother, banishing her to the kitchen with a furious glance. Two weeks ago no boy had ever called Maggie. Now two boys had called her in the same evening.

"I talked to Kocik after school," Matt said without preamble. "Here's the deal. All three judges read all the entries, and they each chose a list of semifinalists. The list of finalists was made up of names that had been on all three semifinalist lists. Then the judges voted to rank the finalists, one, two, three, honorable mention."

"Was I a finalist? Did she say?"

"I could tell she didn't want to talk about it. She sounded sort of nervous, like maybe she wasn't supposed to be talking to me at all. And she said she couldn't give me any specific information about any other student, for privacy reasons. But I figured out it had to be that one of the judges didn't nominate you as a semifinalist, which knocked you out right there, however high the other judges ranked you. In this contest you didn't have a chance unless all three judges picked you out of the pile."

"And one of them didn't pick me." Even though it was painfully obvious who it had to be, neither Matt nor Maggie had said the name.

"It looks that way. Listen, Maggie, you should go talk to Kocik yourself. I can't get any more information out of her, because I'm not you. But if you went to talk to her, I bet she'd tell you something."

Maggie didn't want to talk to Ms. Kocik, but she felt growing in her an overwhelming need to know the truth. "Will you go with me?"

"Sure. After school on Monday?"

"After school on Monday."

. . .

It helped that Ms. Kocik was Maggie's social studies teacher and her second-favorite teacher, after Mr. O. Was Mr. O. still Maggie's favorite teacher? Maggie didn't know. She only knew that she got a lump in her throat every time she thought about how things used to be.

Ms. Kocik was in her mid-forties, Maggie guessed, with frizzy, faded-blond hair and sharp, intelligent eyes.

"Two more intrepid seekers after truth!" she said when Matt and Maggie presented themselves at her classroom door after the final bell. "Come on in, you two." Maggie hardly felt intrepid.

They took seats in the front of the room. Maggie waited for Matt to explain why they were there. He didn't. So, without looking Ms. Kocik in the face, Maggie said, "It's about the essay contest. I know everybody couldn't win. I know lots and lots of people entered, and everything. But—I thought my essay was—well, I really thought it was the best essay I've ever written. And usually my essays turn out pretty well, so I was just wondering . . ." She trailed off.

"I thought your essay was truly outstanding, Maggie," Ms. Kocik said gently. "I would have liked to see it as one of our winners. I don't think I'll be crossing any line I shouldn't cross if I tell you that yours was one on which the judges disagreed, rather vehemently, I might say. And our procedure this year was set up so that no essay could advance to the finalist stage unless all three judges selected it. In hindsight, I think this system didn't end up being a fair one; it gave too much power to any judge who strongly disliked a particular essay, for any reason."

"Was it Mr. O.?" Maggie hadn't expected to put the question so bluntly, but it just came out.

"Oh, Maggie. Try to think of it this way. How old are you, Maggie—twelve?"

"I'm almost thirteen." She'd be thirteen in another two days, to be exact.

"All right, you're almost thirteen, you decide not to do dissections, and you write an essay denouncing animal dissections as immoral. And, by implication, you denounce anyone who does dissections as the moral equivalent of a murderer. Now imagine that you're in your forties, and you've spent twenty years of your life doing dissections and helping others to do them. For twenty years you've thought you were doing something positive, helping others to learn about the hidden mysteries of life. Now someone comes along and condemns this work, condemns *you* as morally monstrous. How would you respond?"

"I wouldn't blackball her essay for a contest because I disagreed with it," Matt said.

How could Matt know what he would do if he were Mr. O.? How could he be so certain that he would always do the right thing? Though maybe he would. After all, Maggie's essay had indirectly denounced Matt, too, and yet he was sitting here beside her.

"All I'm saying is, try to understand," Ms. Kocik said. She got up from her desk. The discussion was clearly over.

"Thank you," Maggie said. "For being willing to talk to us."

"Well, I think it's only fair that you understand. But I'd appreciate it if you didn't repeat anything I said here."

Maggie nodded. Matt looked too angry to speak. Once they were out in the hall, he said, "So much for freedom of speech in Grand Valley Middle School. And now that we know there's no such thing as free speech here, we're supposed to shut up and pretend everything is all hunky-dory. 'Don't repeat anything I said here.' What if we did tell? What if for once people discovered an injustice and *didn't* roll over and play dead?"

"Don't." Maggie's eyes pleaded with Matt. "We *can't* say anything. We'd only get Ms. Kocik in trouble, and she's been so nice to us. Besides, she didn't come right out and say it was Mr. O."

"She all but did. Do you have any reasonable doubt who it was?"

"No," Maggie said softly. Somehow, after talking to Ms. Kocik, she didn't feel angry at Mr. O. anymore, if she ever had. She just felt terribly, terribly sad.

"All right," Matt said. "I won't spill any beans. The absence of any meaningful freedom of speech at Grand Valley Middle School will be our dirty little secret. But one thing I *am* going to do: I'm going to write a letter to Kocik, Bellon, Bealer—and to Mr. O.—and I'm going to refuse their award."

"Are you going to say why?"

"I don't need to," Matt said. "They already know."

High on top of the bleachers after school on Tuesday, Jake and Maggie sat planning the liberation of Froggles. The frog dissection was only three days away.

It was a cold afternoon, overcast, with a raw wind that whipped Maggie's hair against her face. There was probably no windier spot than the top of the bleachers, but that was where they always sat, so that was where they sat now. Jake seemed to share Maggie's strong sense of tradition. Maybe the more some parts of your life changed, the more you wanted other parts to stay the same.

Still, it was cold enough that Maggie could hardly

think for shivering. "It's too windy here," she said. "Let's go sit in our tree."

She didn't have to say which tree. Jake stood up and, still holding on to Maggie's mittened hand, led her down the bleachers. Then, hand in hand, they ran across the street to the park, and Jake boosted Maggie again onto the lowest branch of the tree.

A gust of wind rattled the branch on which they were sitting. "I'm still cold," Maggie said.

For answer, Jake kissed her. Maybe he hadn't kissed her since the first time because they were under some enchantment that required them to perch in the winter-bare branches of an oak tree. Or maybe it was the tree that was enchanted. The wind died down, at least for the moment. Maggie almost expected the sun to come out, and buds to appear on the branches, then burst into new green leaves.

"So," Jake said when they finally pulled apart from each other. "Frogs."

"Frogs," Maggie repeated, trying to focus.

"The only real question is where to hide. The worst place is in the johns. The janitors clean there first. I think our best bet is backstage in the auditorium if nothing else is going on there, which I don't think it is."

"How will we know when to come out?"

"It'll be tricky. The custodians take a dinner break

132

about five-thirty. We can sneak out while they're on break."

"What if one of them sees us?"

Jake shrugged. "Then one of them sees us."

Maggie couldn't see that this plan was any better than the plan of just scooping up Froggles after class when everybody was streaming out of the room and Mr. O. had his back turned. That plan would have been risky; Jake's plan sounded riskier still. But Jake seemed to be drawn to the high drama of an after-school stakeout. Talking about it, he came alive in a way that Maggie hadn't seen before. And if they ended up saving Froggles, it would all be worth it.

Maggie's birthday was Wednesday. She was thirteen—a teenager. She could see the teen years stretching ahead, one after the other: thirteen, fourteen, fifteen, sixteen, seventeen, eighteen, nineteen. She was on her way to being *twenty*. The thought made Maggie feel very old. She couldn't help thinking: That was *it*? *That* had been her *childhood*?

It wasn't just her birthday that made Maggie feel childhood was now behind her. It was everything that had happened in the past few weeks between her and Mr. O. It was thinking people you loved were perfect and then having them turn out to be flawed. Her perfect best friend was a coward; her perfect teacher was unfair. These were the truths Maggie now had to face.

Her mother found Maggie almost in tears when she came in to rouse her for her birthday breakfast.

"Maggles! You can't be sad on your *birthday*. Happy birthday, dearest one."

Maggie hugged her mother tighter than usual. You weren't too old if you could still hug your mother. For breakfast her mother actually made waffles—real waffles on her old waffle iron. They were delicious.

At lunch Alycia presented Maggie with a birthday cupcake and a small square present topped with a large, polka-dotted bow.

"I hope you like it," Alycia said.

Slowly, Maggie unwrapped it, slitting the tape with her fingernail so she could slide the paper off without tearing it. She always felt shy opening gifts in front of the gift-giver.

Inside the wrapping was a small white box. Maggie lifted off the top. There, on a soft bed of white cotton, lay a gold and silver bracelet, simple and beautiful in design, a strand of silver intertwined with a strand of gold.

"I love it!" Maggie put it on her wrist to admire.

Beaming now, Alycia pulled up her sleeve to reveal a matching bracelet on her own wrist. "I got one for me, too. They can be like friendship bracelets. Like, I'm the gold and you're the silver. Or you're the gold and I'm the silver. Whatever. The way they're linked together made me think of friendship. Of you and me."

"I love it," Maggie said again, holding her arm out next to Alycia's.

She did love it. Yet, at the same time, she felt that wearing Alycia's friendship bracelet was a kind of lie. Maggie had so many secrets from Alycia now, secrets that best friends wouldn't keep from each other. Alycia didn't know that Maggie and Matt had checked up on the contest. She didn't know that Maggie and Jake were going to rescue Froggles, or that Jake had held Maggie's hand, and called her on the phone, and kissed her twice. Maggie and Alycia weren't intertwined anymore like gold and silver in a friendship bracelet. They were drifting further apart every day, as two people were bound to drift apart when one was willing to stand up for what she believed in and one . . . wasn't.

13

Maggie had her piano lesson after school that day, so her mother was home before her when Maggie arrived there at five o'clock. They were going out to the Thai restaurant for dinner, for some birthday eggplant and tofu.

As soon as Maggie came into the living room, she could sense from the tension—the anger?—in her mother's face that something was wrong. Had her mother had a fight with Alycia's dad at work? Was Maggie in some kind of trouble she didn't know about? Maggie had a sudden uneasy thought: Had Mr. O. somehow discovered the Froggles plot? But he couldn't have.

"The mail came," her mother said abruptly. "You got a birthday card. From your dear old dad."

As Maggie stood motionless, her mother went on, "Go ahead, open it."

Maggie looked down at the pale green envelope lying on the coffee table. She still recognized her father's handwriting. Even though it had been six years since she had last heard from him, it had been only a few weeks since she had reread the cards hidden in her shoe box.

"I'll go away so you can read it in privacy." Her mother stalked off toward the kitchen.

Maggie picked it up. The same card that was in her hands now had been in her father's hands two days ago. She read the return address: Wayne McIntosh, 2314 Orchid Lane, Silver Spring, Maryland. He had moved sometime in the past six years. The last card had been sent from Ann Arbor, Michigan.

As carefully as she had opened Alycia's present, Maggie broke the seal on the back flap of the envelope and took out the card. It was a pretty one, with a picture of an old-fashioned girl sitting on a bench by a waterfall. The words printed on the front said "Happy Birthday, Daughter."

Inside, she made herself read the printed message first:

> Although we're far apart today
> You're in my heart, you know.

You're always close within my thoughts
However far you go.

But *she* hadn't gone anywhere: *he* was the one who had gone.

Finally, she read the signature: Love, Dad. The other cards had been signed Daddy. In six years Daddy had become Dad. Below he had written, "I miss you. Write to me and tell me how you're doing."

That was it. That was all. Maggie counted his words: fourteen, like birthday candles, one for each year of her life and one for luck.

He wanted her to write to him and tell him how she was doing—but he hadn't told her how he was doing. Did he have other children? Another daughter?

Anger, sudden and sharp, stabbed through Maggie. She would never write to him, never ever ever, not if he came crawling to her across the sands of the Sahara, not if he wrote a ten-page letter to her every day for the rest of her life, not if he left his new life and new wife and new children as cruelly and coldly as he had once left her.

She started to rip the card in half, planning to shred it as violently and savagely as her mother had done the wedding photos from the pages of their album. But at the first tear in the picture of the pretty, old-fashioned girl, Maggie's own heart tore within her. She couldn't rip up this card, not after she had saved the other ones so faithfully, for all these years. She wouldn't write to her father, she couldn't, but she would keep his card in her shoe box with the rest of her pathetic souvenirs. Tears stinging her eyes, Maggie stumbled toward the desk for a piece of tape.

Her mother had come back into the living room. "Oh, Maggie, Maggles, my poor, poor, darling baby." Her mother held her as if she were four years old again and her father had just left. But that time he had left her. This time she was leaving him.

On Thursday, Mr. O. didn't say a word as he handed Maggie her pass to go to the library during Friday's frog dissection. This time he handed one to Jake, too. Maggie waited to see if Alycia would ask for a pass, as well. Of course, she didn't.

Mr. O. gave more details about the pithing procedure. The point of it was supposed to be to cut Froggles's central nervous cord so that they could see exactly how the nerves were connected to the muscles, and how different muscles could be twitched by manipulating different nerves. It sounded even more cruel and barbaric to Maggie this time. Were the others really planning to sit there and *watch* as Mr. O. cut off Froggles's head?

But Froggles wasn't going to be there tomorrow to

have his head snipped off. At least, Maggie hoped he wasn't. The plan seemed fantastic, impossible. How would they pass the long hours until the school was empty enough for them to make their move? Wasn't someone bound to see them loitering so late and give the alarm?

At lunch, Maggie threw away her sandwich, un-eaten. "I'm tired of peanut butter and jelly," she said in response to Alycia's inquiring glance.

"Do you want to share?" Alycia offered, holding out a plastic bag with cookies that the two girls had baked together the previous weekend: thick, chewy cookies with fruity centers.

Maggie shook her head. "I'm not that hungry."

"How was the rest of your birthday?" Alycia asked then.

"All right," Maggie said. She and her mother hadn't mentioned the card again during dinner, and the curried tofu and eggplant had been delicious.

Maggie glanced down at her new bracelet, lying cool and smooth against her wrist. "I got a birthday card from my dad." She had to tell Alycia *something* about her life if they were still pretending to be best friends.

Alycia's eyes widened. "From your dad?" She looked uncertain how she was supposed to respond. Then she said, "That's great! I mean, isn't it?"

"You think so?" The suddenness of her fury caught Maggie off guard. "One card in six years? One card with fourteen words written on it? It doesn't sound that great to me."

"Well, but at least it's something. It shows he still cares about you."

"It doesn't take a lot of caring to buy a dumb card and stick it in a dumb envelope. His new wife probably bought it for him."

Maggie knew it wasn't Alycia's fault that Maggie didn't have a father and Alycia did, but the force of all her accumulated anger was so strong she couldn't stop. "What would you know about it, anyway? You *have* a father. You have everything. And you sure do your best to hang on to it, too."

Alycia looked as if she had been struck. "What are you talking about? Look, Maggie, I didn't mean anything. You're the one who brought it up. You said you got a card from your dad, and I didn't know what to say, so I said the first thing that came into my head. I didn't want to make you mad."

Stop it! A small voice inside Maggie's head commanded her. *Stop it now!*

Instead, she said, "I'm talking about *dissections*. I'm talking about your precious, perfect biology *grade*. You don't care how many animals get pithed, do you? You don't care how many frogs get their heads cut off, so long as *you* get to win the essay contest and *you* get to keep your record of nice, neat straight A's. Isn't there anything that you would stand up for? Isn't there anything that's almost as important to you as being Miss Perfect?"

"If that's what you think of me"—Alycia's voice was trembling—"that all I care about is prizes and grades, then why do you want to be my friend?"

Maggie didn't say anything. Right then she *didn't* want to be friends with someone who was a hypocrite and a coward. She stood up from the table and walked away from the best friend she had ever had.

By eighth-period math, Maggie felt almost physically sick with terror over the imminence of the frognapping with Jake. Her throat felt dry and swollen, even as her palms were wet with clammy perspiration. And all through the afternoon she kept remembering how Alycia's face had crumpled—how she had reduced Alycia, who never cried, to tears.

Too soon the final bell rang. As planned, Maggie and Jake met at Jake's locker. Even Jake looked nervous. He was paler than usual, and his hair needed washing. Maggie felt no desire to brush back his greasy bangs with her sweaty hand.

"The important thing is to act natural," Jake said in a low voice. "You can get away with anything if you act natural. That's how shoplifters get themselves caught: they act like they expect to be pounced on any minute. The plainclothes cops watch them creeping around all jittery and shifty-eyed, and, bingo, they pounce."

Maggie didn't ask how Jake knew so much about the psychology of shoplifters. She concentrated on acting natural, knowing that if there had been any plainclothes cops in Grand Valley Middle School, they would have pounced on her already.

"There's no rehearsal today," Jake said as they walked together toward the auditorium. "I asked in the office."

Maggie couldn't even imagine the nerve it would take to make an inquiry like that in the school office, under these circumstances. *Excuse me, could you tell me if anybody is using the school auditorium today? Because my friend and I want to hide there until the coast is clear and then sneak out and steal the classroom frog from Mr. O.'s room. It's free? Thanks. That's all I wanted to know.* But Jake was obviously better at acting natural than she was.

The auditorium was dark. Maggie and Jake felt for each other's hands. They shuffled down the sloping aisle to the stairs that led up to the stage, then groped their way past the heavy velvet curtains that hid the backstage area from audience view. Maggie's eyes had grown more accustomed to the dark now, and she could dimly make out the shape of a couple of straight-backed chairs, some cardboard cartons, and a heap of drop cloths.

"Here," Jake said. It was the first word either of them had spoken since they entered the auditorium. Jake pulled Maggie down next to him on the soft pile of tangled fabric against the wall. "This isn't too bad."

He kissed Maggie, proving that they weren't bound by magic to kiss only in the oak tree. But this time Jake's kiss lasted too long. Maggie suddenly dreaded the next two hours alone with him in the dark. She pulled away.

"What's the matter?"

Maggie decided to tell the truth. It was easier to tell the truth to someone when you couldn't see his face. "I'm afraid."

"Of me? Of this? Of what we're going to do?"

"Of everything."

"I wouldn't hurt you. I'd never hurt you."

Maggie couldn't believe Jake. She believed that he *believed* what he had said, but she didn't believe that what he had said was true. It wasn't the kind of thing you could promise to someone else. *I'll never hurt you.*

Once she would have thought that she could never hurt Alycia, and yet she had said the most hurtful things she could think of to her a few hours ago. For all Maggie knew, her father had thought the same thing about her and her mother.

"Have you heard from your dad?" Maggie asked. You could ask anybody anything in the darkness.

"Yeah. He called last week."

"Where is he?"

"San Diego."

"What did he say?"

"Nothing."

"Nothing?"

" 'How are you? That's good, I'm fine, too. You know, this doesn't have anything to do with you and me. It has to do with your mother and me. Everything between *us* is still the same. I don't know when I'll be able to call again. Take care of yourself. Bye.' "

Maggie let Jake's words settle. Then she said softly, "My dad left, too."

"You're kidding."

"A long time ago. When I was four. I haven't seen him since. But I got a birthday card from him yesterday."

"Yesterday was your birthday?"

"Uh-huh."

"You didn't tell me. I would have gotten you something."

Maggie tried to think what kind of present Jake would pick out for a girl. "What would you have gotten me?"

"What do you want?"

"A frog."

"Coming right up."

Even though Maggie couldn't see Jake's face, she could tell he was smiling. Then she could feel his smile fade.

"Did your mom ever marry anybody else?" he asked.

"No." Maggie's mom never even dated anybody else. And yet her mother was young, for a mother, and pretty. But Maggie's mother knew how to keep her distance from men. You could tell that she viewed them all as potential Mistake Number Threes.

"Did your dad?" Jake asked.

"Uh-huh."

"Any kids?"

"I don't know. Probably."

"If I ever get married and have kids," Jake said, "I'm never going to leave."

"Me neither."

"I'm not going to get married unless I *know* I can stay forever, and that she'll stay forever."

"Me too." Maggie reached out for Jake's hand and intertwined her fingers with his, to make up for pulling away from his kiss. "On the card? My dad said I should write to him, tell him how I'm doing."

"That was big of him." Jake's scorn was reassuring. Maggie *shouldn't* think it was "great" that her dad had "at least" sent her "something."

"I'm not going to," Maggie said, in case Jake thought she was wavering. "If he wanted to know how I was doing, he shouldn't have left. He probably doesn't care how I'm doing, anyway. It was just something to put on the bottom of the card."

"If my dad calls again, I'm hanging up on him," Jake said. "Not that I expect him to call anytime soon. I'm a pretty low priority in his life right now, compared to the twenty-year-old babe he left me and my mom for." Jake's grip tightened on Maggie's hand. "I hate his guts, Maggie. I hate what he did to my mom. I even hate myself for having half my genes from him."

"That doesn't mean you're anything like him," Maggie said softly, hoping it was true.

"We look the same. I want to spit in the mirror sometimes, my face looks so much like his."

"I like the way your face looks."

It came out sounding like a cue for a kiss. But Jake didn't kiss Maggie again. All he said was "Yeah. You like everything, though. Having you like me doesn't count."

Maggie didn't contradict him. The conversation had

turned too sad, almost scary. She didn't want to talk anymore about Jake's dad, but other topics seemed silly and shallow after the things Jake had said.

For a long time they waited side by side in silence, leaning up against the hard cement-block wall. Jake's breathing was so slow and regular that Maggie wondered if he had fallen asleep. She came close enough to sleep herself that Jake's voice seemed to call her back from a great distance.

"It's five-thirty."

"How do you know?" Maggie had lost all sense of time.

Jake held out his glow-in-the-dark watch. "The custodians should be on break now. It sounds pretty quiet out there."

Hand in hand, Maggie and Jake retraced their steps and slowly pushed open the heavy auditorium door to the hall. The lights were off, except for the two security lights that glowed at both ends of the long corridor. The silence itself seemed to make a sound, the sound of an enormously quiet, pulsating presence.

Upstairs in Mr. O.'s room, they had to turn on the lights. The sudden brightness made Maggie feel exposed, caught in the accusing beam of a policeman's spotlight. If the custodians walked by, they would notice the light right away. Not that a stray light in a classroom was all that suspicious. Perhaps some teacher had returned to school to work late. Did teachers ever come back to school in the evening to work alone in their rooms?

Did Mr. O.?

"Hurry," Maggie whispered urgently, not that they needed to whisper when there was no one else in the room to hear.

Froggles gave one small croak. "Hush!" Maggie told him. Jake held open the sack as Maggie reached into the terrarium and lifted out the frog. "Everything's all right now," Maggie told him softly. "You're not going to be pithed tomorrow."

She turned to Jake. "Let's go." If you could shout in a whisper, Maggie was shouting.

Jake made no move to leave. "There's no hurry. I want to look around."

Deliberately, Jake sauntered over to Mr. O.'s desk and sat down. He opened Mr. O.'s drawers, one by one.

"Here's a picture of him with his wifey-poo." To Maggie's horror, Jake spat at it, the way he had talked about spitting in the mirror. The sight of the thick gob of spittle dribbling down the glass of the frame turned Maggie's stomach.

"*Don't.* We have no right to touch his things."

"Says who?"

"Says me!"

"He has a right to murder frogs, he has a right to screw you over for your contest, but we have no right to spit in his face?"

"I want to go!" Maggie pulled at Jake's arm. He shook her off, his face dark with anger now, as if it were her fault that he hated Mr. O., hated his father, hated himself.

"No one's stopping you."

Maggie didn't know if she was more afraid of walking out through the dim, silent halls by herself or of leaving Jake alone to do—whatever he was going to do.

"Jake, *please.*"

"I'm not through."

Finally Jake got up from Mr. O.'s desk. He walked over to the windowsill, where all the classroom microscopes sat lined up in an orderly row.

"Do you want a microscope?" Jake asked Maggie.

"No!"

"Neither do I."

Jake leaned over the sill and pushed up the second-story window. A surge of icy wind stung Maggie's flaming cheeks.

"Bye-bye, microscope," Jake said, in a voice more chilling for being so cheerful.

Maggie tried to drag Jake away from the window,

but he was too strong for her. He sent the microscope crashing to the pavement below. Maggie heard herself scream.

"Jake! Maggie! What is going on here?"

There, in the classroom doorway, stood Mr. O.

14

Maggie hurled herself into Mr. O.'s arms. She wouldn't have blamed him if he had pushed her away. But he didn't. He held her close, her face pressed against his jacket, her cheek squashed against the cool metal of the zipper tab.

"What is going on here?" Mr. O. repeated. This time he was speaking only to Jake. "One of the custodians called me and asked if I had any students doing work for me after hours. Believe me, I was over here in three minutes flat."

When Jake didn't answer, Mr. O. released Maggie and turned her toward him so he could see her face.

"We wanted to save Froggles," Maggie whispered in a choked voice. "But then . . ."

"Then our young vandal here, whose protests

against dissection were never very convincing, decided to use this as an opportunity to destroy valuable school property. Is that right?"

It was right, and it wasn't right. Jake *had* cared about saving Froggles—or at least Maggie hoped he had. Right now she wasn't certain about anything. Jake had so much anger in him, about so much more than dissections.

"Saving him was my idea," Maggie whispered. The least she could do for Jake was take her fair share of the blame.

"I'm sure it was." Mr. O. quickly scanned the room. "And rifling through my desk and vandalizing school property was *his* idea."

"So what are you going to do? Call our fathers?" Jake gave a short, hard laugh.

"I'm going to call your parents, yes. And then I'm going to call the police."

"You think I'm going to stick around for that? I'm outta here, mister." Jake gave one last, anguished look at Maggie, and then he bolted from the classroom, leaving the sack with Froggles in it, still plaintively croaking, behind him on Mr. O.'s desk.

Mr. O. didn't run after him. "I'm not chasing any teenaged punks," he said, as much to himself as to Maggie. "He isn't going to get far."

Maggie waited for Mr. O. to pick up the phone on his

desk. Instead he sat down on top of one of the lab tables and motioned to Maggie to sit on the table facing him.

"Maggie." The old kindness was back in his voice, mixed with a new pain. "How'd a sweet kid like you get mixed up with a creep like him?"

A *creep*. It was the same word Jake had used to describe Mr. O. And, as she had that other time, Maggie said, "He's not a creep. He's just upset about a lot of other stuff in his life." She hesitated, then said, "His dad left, too."

"That doesn't justify what happened here tonight."

Maggie knew that it didn't.

"Are you ready to drop this dissection thing now? Maggie, I realize you feel deeply about this. When you're young, you feel deeply about a lot of things. But feeling is one thing, acting is another. Your actions tonight—look what they led to. A valuable microscope has been destroyed. I'll have to file a police report on both of you—required procedure for any destruction of school property. You'll almost certainly get some kind of suspension. Tell me, Maggie, was it worth it?"

A police report. Suspension. The magnitude of the punishment that she was facing overwhelmed her: Maggie McIntosh, teacher's pet, had never even had a detention. And Froggles was going to be slaughtered, anyway. If only Jake had taken the sack with him when he fled. What if Maggie seized it and ran? But she couldn't, now that Mr. O. was talking to her again as if what happened to her really mattered to him. Yet she couldn't give up her fight against dissections, either.

"I don't know," Maggie said, her voice coming out stronger and more sure than she had thought it would. "I still think it's wrong to kill animals."

"I'm afraid I disagree."

"My essay—for the contest—"

"You think I didn't vote for your essay because I took issue with its conclusions. Believe me, Maggie, I bent over backward to be fair. I probably rated your essay too highly because I was so careful to correct for what might be bias against your point of view. But in the end, I didn't think your arguments were very good ones. I'm sorry, Maggie. I had to vote according to my own best judgment."

Did he believe what he was saying? If he didn't, he was lying to Maggie, but if he did, he was deceiving himself. Maggie knew now, as surely as she had ever known anything in her life, that Mr. O. *had* been unfair. He had treated her unfairly, both in the judging of the contest and in the overly harsh penalties for her conscientious refusal to dissect. Mr. O. had told her that if she didn't do dissections, she'd leave him no choice but to fail her. But that, too, was a lie. If other teachers let students do simulated dissections on the computer, or watch dissection videos, why couldn't Mr. O.? If other teachers could teach biology without forcing students to violate their consciences, why couldn't he?

"You're really going to pith Froggles." Maggie said it as a statement, but she meant it as a question.

"Painlessly, Maggie. I'd say that he's a heck of a lot more upset in that sack right now than he's going to be at any point tomorrow. Want to help me put him back where he's more comfortable?"

Maggie shook her head. It was better to be cramped and crowded in a sack on the way to freedom than to luxuriate in your own private cell on death row.

Mr. O.'s face registered disappointment at her refusal, but his disappointment didn't wrench Maggie's heart the way it once had. She was as disappointed in him as he was in her.

As if sensing the unspoken change between them, Mr. O. got up from his perch and began pacing in the front of the room.

"Maggie," he finally said, "I have to continue to give you failing grades for the dissections. But it doesn't seem fair to fail you for the whole trimester. Maybe you can write an extra-credit report to make up for the labs. Would you be willing to do that?"

"Yes," Maggie said over the lump in her throat. Did he really not remember that Maggie herself had suggested this two weeks ago and he had refused? "Thank you," she made herself say. She knew that, for her sake, Mr. O. was going as far as he could.

Even further.

"Oh, Maggie." Mr. O. put his hands on her shoulders and looked into her tear-filled eyes. "Does all this really mean so much to you?" He must have thought she was still thinking about dissections; he didn't know that her tears now weren't only for Froggles but for her, and for Mr. O., and for what they had once had and could never have again.

He turned away from Maggie, staring toward the chalkboard as if memorizing every name in the Light Bulb Hall of Fame. Then, slowly, he picked up the sack with Froggles in it. "This isn't fair to the rest of your classmates, but—here."

Mr. O. pulled out Froggles and held him on the palm of his hand. "Take him. Set him free, turn him into a pet, let him sleep on your pillow. He's yours. I only hope your classmates won't get cheated out of other chances to do this kind of experiment."

Mr. O. dropped Froggles into Maggie's outstretched hand. She cupped her other hand around him, joyfully, protectively, so he couldn't hop away.

"And now," Mr. O. said, "I have to call your mother."

It felt like the middle of the night, but it was only six-thirty when Maggie's mother arrived at school to get her. The school was locked, so Maggie and Mr. O. were waiting outside for her in the parking lot.

Mr. O. drew Maggie's mother aside, out of Maggie's hearing. Maggie didn't know what he was telling her, but she couldn't imagine that it was anything that would particularly gladden her heart after a long, hard day at the university.

"All right, Maggie, let's go" was all her mother said once the conference was over. She sounded infinitely weary.

"I'm sorry," Maggie said in a small voice as she slid into the passenger seat. She could still hear Jake's voice echoing in her ears. *Do you want a microscope? . . . Neither do I . . . Bye-bye, microscope.* And then the sickening sound of the crash . . .

"So what do you have to say for yourself?" her mother asked.

"I didn't know it would turn out like this," Maggie said. "I just didn't want Froggles to get killed."

Maggie felt for Froggles, safe in her pocket. She hoped he hadn't made any frog poop in there during the long wait for her mother. Despite everything that had happened, Maggie was fiercely, triumphantly glad that she had saved him. Saving Froggles was the one thing Maggie wasn't sorry about.

"Did Mr. O. tell you that he has to report this to the

police? And that you're probably going to get suspended?"

Maggie turned away so her mother wouldn't see how close she was to tears.

"I was right about Jake," her mother said with grim satisfaction. "I don't want you to see him anymore."

"I don't want to see him, either," Maggie whispered. And she didn't. *Had* Jake ever cared about Froggles? Had he ever cared about *her*? Or had he seized upon the rescue as a way to vent his rage?

They rode the rest of the way home in silence. Maggie could feel the tension between them easing. Maggie's mother had stayed angry at Maggie's father for more than eight long years, but she never stayed angry at Maggie. The love between them was a deep, wide sea which anger could barely ripple.

"He gave me Froggles," Maggie said as her mother parked the car in front of their house. She held out her palm, with Froggles perched on it, blinking in the glow of the streetlamp overhead.

"The frog?" her mother said, as if to verify the implausible evidence of her senses.

"Can I keep him? For a pet?"

Maggie's mother had never let her have a pet. She said it was hard enough being the single mother of one human child, let alone of various members of the animal kingdom. And she had every right to refuse to let Maggie keep Froggles as part of her punishment. But Maggie didn't think her mother would grudge Froggles a home now that he was there, looking up at them so hopefully.

"Companion animal," her mother said.

Maggie looked at her blankly.

"You can't say *pet* anymore. According to people at the university. The new, politically correct term is *companion animal*."

Maggie pressed her plea: "So can I keep him?"

Her mother sighed. "All right. What do frogs eat? Are they allowed to eat real bugs, or do we have to find bugs made out of soybeans?"

The phone was ringing when Maggie and her mother walked in the door. Maggie didn't want to pick it up, but she did.

"Maggie."

It was Jake. Maggie had known it would be. "I can't talk to you." Whatever her relationship had been with Jake, it was over.

"I don't expect you to. I just wanted to say—Maggie, you have to know I didn't mean for you to get into trouble. Did Mr. O. call your mom? What are they going to do to you?"

"He called her. I think I'm going to be suspended."

"He called my mom, too. Like I care about getting suspended. But what kills me is that we have to pay for the microscope, and my mom and I are not really rolling in dough right now. And he said I have to go to counseling. The school has some kind of special program for juvenile delinquents." Jake gave his familiar mirthless laugh.

"Jake?"

"What?"

"I'm never going to forget you. Being with you. In the tree. Not ever."

That was all Maggie said. But she knew Jake knew it was goodbye.

Her mother called to her from the kitchen, where she was fixing a temporary terrarium for Froggles. "Was that Mr. Tofu? He called before."

"Matt. No. What did *he* want?"

"He didn't say."

Maggie reached for the phone. She was going to call Matt. But there was someone else she had to call first.

Alycia answered the phone on the second ring.

"Alycia, it's me, Maggie. I'm sorry. I'm really truly sorry. I shouldn't have said those things. I mean, you're you, and I'm me, and you don't have to fight for the same things I fight for. And I hope you'll be my friend again, though I'll understand if you won't. Especially now that I'm going to be suspended from school. But I hope you will."

There was a pause at the other end of the line. Maybe Alycia didn't want to be friends anymore. Maggie really couldn't blame her if she didn't. But it was hard to imagine what life would be like without Alycia to bake with and knit with and share hot chocolate with as they sat side by side doing homework.

"*Suspended?*" Alycia asked.

Maggie told her the story.

"I didn't know you were that involved with Jake," Alycia said slowly.

"I felt funny telling people about him. I should have told you. But you never seemed to like him very much—though I guess you were right not to like him. But I just . . . *did* like him."

"Listen, who you like is up to you. You can like whoever you want to like," Alycia said. "And, anyway, a lot of the things you said about me were true. I *don't* have guts. Not like you. You stand up for what you believe in. I don't."

"You *could*," Maggie said. She didn't say it to put pressure on Alycia. She was through with expecting people to be who she wanted them to be. But guts were something anybody could have, who chose to have them. In that way, guts were different from, say, fathers.

"You mean, refuse to do the dissection tomorrow."

"I'm not saying you *should*. I'm saying you *could*."

There was another long pause. Then, "Maybe," Alycia said. Maggie knew that *maybe* meant *maybe not*. But that was suddenly all right, too. Alycia might not have guts, but she was honest enough to admit that she didn't—and forgiving enough to welcome back a friend who had said some cruel things to her in anger.

Maggie felt shy as she picked up the phone to return Matt's call. She had never called a boy before.

When Matt answered, he, too, sounded uncharacteristically hesitant, not at all like the Matt who was so sure about everything and everybody. "I was wondering—well, I checked at the library, and they have videos of dissections. Of all the dissections we're doing in class. I thought maybe if you watched them, you'd get the experience of looking inside an animal without having to kill it or anything. And I could kind of explain things to you as we watched. *If* you wanted to. Watch one of the videos. Sometime. With me."

Maggie almost laughed. Was Matt asking her for a *date*? To watch an *animal dissection video*? It was so sweet, as well as so ridiculous, that Maggie hardly knew what to say. But Alycia's father had said that videos were a good alternative to live animal dissections. Maybe Mr. O. would count watching them as makeup credit in biology.

Matt was opinionated, arrogant, intellectually bullying—but he had taken her side in the essay contest and had given up his own prize to protest an injustice that he felt strongly about. And he really wanted to find a way for her to share the excitement he felt about science.

"Sure," Maggie said, as brightly as she could manage. "I'd like that."

"Sometime this weekend? I could bring one over to your house. Like tomorrow night? At seven o'clock?"

"Which one?"

"I thought we could start with the worm."

Maggie envisioned a series of Friday night dates: worm, fish, frog. She'd put Froggles's terrarium in another room during the frog video. And she could make some microwave popcorn to munch as they watched.

Maggie sat smiling to herself as she hung up the phone. For everything you lost in life, there was something you gained. Maggie had lost Jake and Mr. O. She had gained Matt and Froggles. She had lost Alycia, and she had gained her back again. She knew the friendship would be different, but she hoped it could be deeper and truer than before.

And her father? Maggie still didn't know why he had left her and her mother. No explanation could justify what he had done. But it had to have taken courage for him to send the card. He had to be waiting to see if she would write back. Maggie didn't want to be like Jake, consumed with hatred and rage. In a way, Maggie *had* been given a choice whether or not to have a father. She wanted to choose to have one.

Maggie found her mother in her bedroom, lying on the bed that she hadn't shared with anybody for the last eight years.

"Mom?"

"Maggles?"

"Would you mind if I wrote to him?" Maggie wasn't going to write to her father if it hurt her mother, she knew that much. "On the card, he said I should write to him and let him know how I'm doing."

There was a long silence. Maggie could see the anger rising in her mother's face.

"You *want* to write to him? You think he *deserves* to know how you're doing?"

"No. But sort of. I mean, I sort of do want to write to him. I don't think he deserves anything. But it's like, he *is* my father. You guys must have loved each other once, at least a little bit, even if you hate each other now. So—would you mind if I wrote to him? I'm not going to do it if you don't want me to."

"Oh, Maggles." Maggie's mother tossed her a pillow. Maggie lay down on the bed, on her mother's patchwork quilt, with her head at the bottom of the bed and her feet at the top, facing her mother. "If you want to write to him, write to him."

"You mean it?"

"I mean it. I don't know, maybe Mistake Number Three is to hold on to bitterness. That's what I've been doing, for lo these many years." Her mother spoke so softly that Maggie had to strain to hear her. "But he's lost more than I have. I just lost him. But he lost you."

Maggie reached for her mother's hand and gave it a tight squeeze. She loved her mother more than she could put into words. She wouldn't trade her mother for all the pita-pocket sandwiches in the world.

She slipped away to her own room and took out a piece of flower-edged stationery from her bottom desk drawer. Then she pulled out a whole stack of it.

"Dear Dad," she wrote, staring down at the unfamiliar words as they appeared on the page. "You said to write, so I'm writing. But you had better write back! A lot has happened in eight years. Maybe the first thing I should tell you is that I have a companion amphibian now. His name is Froggles."